Nearly
Departed

Nearly Departed

Welcome to Weirdsville...

ROOK HASTINGS

HarperCollins *Children's Books*

First published in Great Britain by HarperCollins *Children's Books* 2010

HarperCollins *Children's Books* is a division of HarperCollins*Publishers* Ltd
77-85 Fulham Palace Road, Hammersmith, London W6 8JB

www.harpercollins.co.uk

1

ISBN: 978 0 00 725810 9

Typeset in Times by Palimpsest Book Production Limited,
Grangemouth, Stirlingshire

Printed and bound in England by
Clays Ltd, St Ives plc

Mixed Sources

Product group from well-managed
forests and other controlled sources
www.fsc.org Cert no. SW-COC-1806
© 1996 Forest Stewardship Council

FSC is a non-profit international organisation established to promote the
responsible management of the world's forests. Products carrying the FSC
label are independently certified to assure consumers that they come
from forests that are managed to meet the social, economic and
ecological needs of present and future generations.

Find out more about HarperCollins and the environment at
www.harpercollins.co.uk/green

WELCOME ✠O "WEIRDSVILLE"

Kevin Carter tucked his chin into the neck of his hoody as he walked his Staffordshire bull terrier one cold January night. He hated walking that dog, but his mum told Carter she'd have his guts if Billy did his business in the flat one more time, and Carter's mum was pretty much the only thing in the world that he was afraid of.

Breath billowed out of his nose, steaming in the freezing air, and he thrust his hands deeper into his jeans pockets, Billy's lead looped over his wrist. With any luck he'd get the mangy mutt to do what he had to on the scrub grass under the main overpass into town. His mum'd told him that if he insisted on buying a dog out of the back of a van then he would have to look after it properly, take it for walks down to the park or the woods outside town where it could get some proper exercise.

But Carter had only bought Billy to enhance his image

as local gang leader and hard man; he wasn't going to spend his life running round after the dumb animal. Besides, it got so dark really early this time of year. And while Carter wasn't afraid of anything, and most things were afraid of him, if he ever stopped to think why he didn't like hanging around alone at night, he would have come to the conclusion that the night seemed to belong here in Woodsville more than any other place on earth.

Anyway, the park was supposed to shut at dusk, mostly because of the gangs and the dealers that Carter spent a lot of his time hanging out with. And he'd stopped taking Billy there since he'd tried to set him up to fight Greg Winter's illegal pit bull, when Billy had proper shamed him by running away. Carter had intended to ditch the dog that night, going home without bothering to look for him. But when he got back to his flat, he found Billy waiting on the doorstep, panting gormlessly.

No, Billy would have to make do with a quick sniff and a run about in the thicket of trees and shrubs that filled the deep gully that ran under the road. With a bit of luck, the mutt would dash in front of a car and get run over.

"Go on then, dog breath," Carter growled, stepping off the pavement on to the slick, wet grass, deciding to wait there for Billy rather than descending into the trees. "And hurry up. I got places to be."

Carter expected Billy to twist off his lead with his usual

gleeful jump and rush off into the thicket, as he normally did whenever Carter got bullied into taking him out. After all, he'd been stuck indoors for the best part of a week and had literally jumped for joy when Carter reluctantly hooked the chain lead on to his studded collar just twenty minutes earlier.

But Billy did not move. He stood there, staring into the dense, dark wasteland, one paw hovering just above the freezing ground, nose quivering, sensing something in the air.

"Get on with it," Carter told him impatiently, giving Billy a swift kick in the ribs to get him going. He could be in the pub now, chatting up that barmaid who reckoned she didn't fancy him.

Billy yelped in pain, but instead of running off he took two cautious steps backwards, a low, whining growl rising from deep in his throat. He cowered against Carter's legs.

"What, you bloody poof?" Carter asked the dog. His voice sounded very loud, as if it were echoing off the mist that had begun to rise around his feet. Despite himself, he felt his heartbeat quicken in his chest and realised that the goosebumps prickling on his arms and the back of his neck under his hoody weren't due to the cold. It took Carter a moment to recognise the unfamiliar emotion, but then he realised what it was. He was frightened.

Perhaps Billy wasn't such a waste of space after all;

perhaps he could sense something out there in the dark that Carter couldn't. Maybe one of the rival gangs had followed him and was waiting down in the thicket to take him out. Or maybe there were addicts, looking for a way to pay for their next fix. Normally no one in their right mind would lay a finger on Carter – not if they wanted to have any fingers left the next day – but addicts were hardly ever in their right mind.

Then Carter remembered a story that his mother used to tell him when he was a little kid, to try and keep him in line. It was about the Woodsville murderer who had once stalked the streets of the town looking for his next victim. For a whole year, Carter's mum had told him, the child-killer had terrorised the area, slaughtering one kid a month, always on the fifteenth day and then… he'd simply vanished, never to be heard of again. The police never identified him and no one found out why he stopped killing, but according to Carter's mum, her voice dark with menace, he had vowed to come back, especially for really naughty boys. Then Carter had stopped believing in the bogeyman and she locked him in the understairs cupboard instead.

"OK, you had your chance." Carter shuddered as he bent to hook Billy's lead back on, shaking the clammy memory away. Reminding himself of exactly who he was; the bloke that other people didn't want to bump into on a dark night, not a little kid who was afraid of the dark and his mum's temper.

"Come on then!" But Billy would not budge. No matter how hard Carter tried to drag him back, the dog stood stock-still, staring into the darkness and whimpering.

And then Carter saw something in the bushes, not a man but… a light, yes, it was a light. Like a torch only brighter – a lantern or something – flickering between the trees, casting long, silvery fingers that seemed to reach towards him.

"What the…?" Carter took a step forward and peered into the trees. "Hello? Who's there?" He looked around. The road behind him was deserted and even the windows of the nearby houses were shuttered and dim.

"What, you lost or something?" Carter bellowed, the tension in his tone belying its bravado. He wasn't sure where the question came from; it hadn't been what he'd meant to say, but suddenly his stomach had lurched and he felt lost himself, as if he might never see home again. It was as if everything and everyone he had ever known had vanished; he was all alone in this gully, and he always would be. Carter swore under his breath, struggling to control the raft of unfamiliar emotions that had unexpectedly engulfed him.

"Pull yourself together, you baby." Carter repeated the words his mother had often spoken to him. Then the street light behind him blinked off, leaving him in total darkness under a starless sky, apart from the light in the thicket that seemed to flare and brighten at that exact moment.

Then the scream came. It tore through Carter, pushing him backwards with its force, so that he staggered and struggled to keep his balance. Billy chose this moment to unfreeze and he bucked backwards, in the direction of the estate, wrenching so hard on his lead that pain shot through Carter's arm. The scream filled his head; it vibrated in his chest, pounding at his ribcage and pressing down on his furiously beating heart with the weight of its despair. Then, as violently and suddenly as it had begun, it stopped. And even though he had *felt* the scream in every part of his body, Carter knew that he hadn't *heard* anything – there had been no sound at all. The whole place was deadly silent.

"Gotta go," Carter whispered, his words forming clouds in the cold air. But before he could move, the light from the thicket rushed at him, speeding through the trees, tearing branches off as it approached. Carter froze to the spot; he couldn't move to avoid the onslaught no matter how hard he tried.

Terrified, he closed his eyes and dragged his hands over his ears, trying to block out the silent screaming that had started again, intensifying with the light. Carter felt power-less against whatever it was that was coming at him. As the light engulfed him, he became filled with fear and sadness, and the terror of knowing that there was no one in the whole world he could turn to any more and nowhere that he wanted to be except home.

"I have to get home," Carter heard inside his head. *"Help me get home."*

And then it stopped. Gingerly, Carter opened first one eye and then the other. The bone-cracking cold ebbed away, making the January night seem almost spring-like by comparison. All the feelings of fear and loneliness went too. No, it was more than that; it was as if they had never existed at all. Even the street light was now shining brightly behind him and a stream of traffic roared by on the over-pass, constant and steady.

Billy yapped and tugged at his lead, asking to be let off for a run.

Carter looked into the thicket. Never had a few bushes and trees seemed less menacing. He almost wanted to laugh out loud, so great was his relief.

"Well, go on then, get on with it," he said, unhooking the chain again. He felt a small wave of affection – the first since the dog's shameful behaviour with Greg Winter's pit bull. He took a deep breath as he watched Billy dash headlong into the trees, his tail wagging energetically.

"Must have overdone it last night," Carter told himself. "Must have had one too many of Barry's homebrew."

But even as he put Billy back on the lead and turned towards the estate, one last doubt gnawed away at the back of his mind. That voice, the one that had said it needed to get back home. It wasn't his.

CHAPTER ONE

"*Hamlet*!" Mr Bacon said.

The class groaned as one. Jay Romero sat back in his chair and glanced around at the other kids. Mr Bacon was kidding himself if he thought he was going to get anything out of them now. It was last period and almost dark outside. There was a big inter-school football match after lessons. No one here cared about *Hamlet*, including Jay, who was more academic than most of them. He could do the work, but all that poetry did his head in.

"Is it about a pig, sir? Ham-let – is it?" Kelly King piped up from the back. Most of the girls laughed and all of the boys moaned, working on the general principle that no girl was ever funny. Not even Kelly King, who most of them fancied and feared simultaneously.

"Sir?" Hashim Malik added. "If it's about pigs, I can't read it. It's against my religion. I'll have to be excused."

Mr Bacon pursed his lips and stroked his beard. Jay wondered if he was counting backwards from ten in his head. Mr Bacon had a long fuse. It took far longer to wind him up than some of the other teachers.

"Actually, Kelly," Mr Bacon said, choosing to ignore Hashim, "it's about a *ghost*!"

"Oooooooh!" the class chorused, making sarcastic, wide, scared eyes at each other.

At her desk near the back of the room by the window, Bethan Carpenter sighed and sank lower into her chair. She knew that *Hamlet* was actually about the descent into madness, and that the ghost was probably just a metaphor. But she supposed Mr Bacon had to do something to get the rabble's attention and talk of a ghost was far more likely to do that than anything intelligent. Her classmates were so boringly predictable. She rolled her eyes and looked at her reflection in the window. Her transparent counterpart seemed eerily distant, staring back at her with hollow skull eyes.

"Hamlet is a Prince of Denmark…" Mr Bacon went on with dogged determination.

"Sir, isn't that where bacon comes from?" Hashim tried again. "Is that where you come from, sir? Are you Danish Bacon?"

The back of the class erupted into a series of snorts and oinks, and the front half collapsed into laughter. Mr Bacon stood perfectly still and waited for the din to die away. "A prince who," he continued wearily, "comes home to find his father dead and his mother married to his uncle. And then two of his friends tell him they've seen the ghost of his father. They take Hamlet to see the ghost, who says he's been murdered. Now Hamlet is already grieving for his father and upset that his mother has remarried in less than a month, so he's already suspicious. Who wouldn't be, right?"

The class remained silent, some transfixed by their desk tops, others with their eyes on the clock behind Mr Bacon's head, willing the hands to move just a little faster, anything to get them out of there.

"The question is, were the friends telling the truth or were they mistaken, possibly even drunk? And does Hamlet really see the ghost, or is it a figment of his own grief and increasing delusion?"

Bethan stuck up her hand.

"He's boring, sir, that's what he is," Hashim said. "Can't we read something interesting, sir, written in real words?"

"What, like Wayne Rooney's autobiography?" Mr Bacon asked him scathingly.

"No, sir, I'm better at football than him any day," Hashim said, a fact which he sincerely believed. And it was true that he did seem to be able to win every match the school played almost single-handedly.

"Let's talk about context," Mr Bacon tried again.

"Did you say sex, sir?" Kelly shouted. Even the boys laughed this time.

"After all," Mr Bacon said. "AFTER ALL, Shakespeare's time was very different from our own. In those days they were much more religious, much more pious. They truly believed in the devil, in witchcraft, alchemy and in ghosts. But we don't believe in ghosts today, do we?"

"Actually, sir?" Jay stuck up his hand. "That's not quite true."

Bethan, finally forced to concede that they had about as much chance of really talking about *Hamlet* as she did of bumping into an actual ghost, put down her hand and slumped in her chair. She glanced at her other self on the opposite side of the glass. The only person in the whole of Woodsville who got her was her. Even her mum and dad, who she really loved and who really loved her, didn't get her. They were too busy buying lottery tickets and playing bingo to notice how stifled she felt.

Bethan longed to find a place where people actually cared about Shakespeare, and art, and literature, and proper music. In less than a year's time, as soon as she was sixteen, she intended to pack her bags and do just that. Bethan couldn't wait to get out of Woodsville, to prove that the nagging fear that she would never leave this dump was all in her head.

She smiled a tiny, resigned smile at her image in the window; but somehow her ghostly double did not reflect it back, only looked at her as if it were just as tired of her as she was of everybody else.

"I read it online, sir." Jay's voice interrupted Bethan's thoughts, tearing her eyes away from the image and back to the rest of the class. "A recent survey showed that one in ten Britons claim to have seen or experienced a ghost at one time or another. That's quite a lot of people with nothing to gain from lying, sir, don't you think? Some scientists think that one day there will be evidence to show there is some truth to ghosts and that consciousness might survive death. And we all know that energy can't be destroyed, don't we?" The class and Mr Bacon looked blank. "Well, it can't. After we die, the energy we used to live transforms into something else. We just don't know what."

"Worm food?" Hashim said, winking at one of the girls. All the girls giggled except Kelly. Kelly made it her business never to be impressed by Hashim. Somebody had to.

"So anyway," Jay finished, glancing at Kelly, who was studying her fingernails intently, "maybe the energy of the mind does live on after death, for a little while at least. Maybe longer if the geographical conditions are right. Electromagnetic fields and the like."

"Yes, well," Mr Bacon said, observing how the class, as always, listened to Jay's distraction tactics much more attentively than they ever did to him. "A lot of people claim to have been abducted by aliens, but we don't believe *that*, do we?" He grinned round at the class, but not one of them cracked a smile in return.

"Actually, sir," Jay said again, happy to push his luck as the clock ticked on. "Given the size of the universe, it is *far* more likely that there is other intelligent life out there than not. If it's really just us lot, well then, *that's* strange."

"Well, as long as there's intelligent life *somewhere*." Mr Bacon folded his arms and looked at Jay. "But we're not talking about aliens, are we, Jay?" he said firmly. "We're talking about ghosts, so let's focus, people, shall we? In the sixteenth century most people believed ghosts were real. Why do you think that is?"

The class could not have cared less, especially Kelly who had actually taken a make-up mirror from her bag and was reapplying her eyeliner.

"OK," Mr Bacon said on an inward breath. "Do any of you, in this age of technological wonders, the internet, powered flight and space stations, believe in ghosts? Have any of you sophisticated, supposedly intelligent young people ever seen a ghost? Exac—"

Mr Bacon's rhetorical question was cut short by a flicker from the overhead lighting and the extraordinary sight of a hand rising hesitantly. He was surprised to see that it belonged to Emily Night, who never said anything.

Emily was usually so quiet that she barely even raised her head, let alone her hand. It was as if she were too terrified to move in case somebody noticed her, so most of the time she was nearly invisible. Now here she was getting ready to speak. Despite himself, Mr Bacon was filled with dread on Emily's behalf. For some kids, fading into the background was the best place to be and Emily was one of them.

"Yes, Emily?" he said warily, wondering what on earth she was going to say. He was right to be worried.

"I've seen a ghost, sir," Emily said. "Well, not seen one exactly – but I've heard one. At least, I *think* I have."

There was a moment of stunned disbelief. None of the other thirty-one pupils could believe that Emily Night had just gone and landed herself totally in it.

"You are *so* mental." Kelly's insult was the first to break the silence.

"You stinking nutter," another one joined in. "You haven't heard a ghost – that's just the voices in your head, moron!"

"She should be in a home," one of the boys said. "Shouldn't she, sir? In special needs!"

"That's enough!" Mr Bacon's protest went unheard or at least unheeded.

The chorus of insults went on, led mainly by Kelly King who, once she got going, was very hard to stop.

Jay looked over at Kelly, who had half risen in her chair,

her grey eyes flashing like lightning in her smooth brown face, her long black curls slicked back with gel into a tight ponytail that jiggled and bounced playfully as she shouted at Emily.

He sighed, wishing Kelly was a little bit less terrifying. It would be one hundred per cent easier to fancy her if she didn't frighten him so much. But everyone knew what she was like, and if – like Emily Night – you were stupid enough to attract her scorn then you probably deserved what you got. Kelly wouldn't hesitate to take you down. She never did.

Emily cowered in her seat, apparently trying to shrink into the painted brick wall behind her.

"THAT IS ENOUGH!" Mr Bacon finally raised his voice above the racket. He rounded on Hashim. "One more word from you and you can forget football tonight."

Hashim's eyes widened with disbelief at the injustice and he flung himself back in his chair, making its legs skid audibly over the floorboards. "It wasn't me, sir. I didn't say anything to the spangle!"

"One. More. Word," Mr Bacon said, quietly threatening now. He knew that Hashim was not scared of him. But he also knew that all Hashim cared about was football. And if Mr Bacon had a word with his coach then he'd be dropped, even if it meant losing the inter-school cup. And while that might not be exactly fair, Mr Bacon knew that if he could control Hashim, he had half a chance of controlling the class.

Hashim clamped his lips shut and jutted out his chin in defiance. As Mr Bacon had hoped, the rest of the class followed his lead and near silence was reinstated.

"I will NOT have that kind of behaviour in my class, do you understand?" Mr Bacon said, glancing at Emily, who had almost succeeded in trying to make herself disappear, shrinking her already diminutive form to nearly nothing. Smaller than most, and without any of the trendy clothes the rest of the kids seemed to rank their status by, she'd always languished at the bottom of the class. Mr Bacon realised he was just as guilty of looking right through her as the kids were.

"Everyone has a right to speak. *If* one in ten people are supposed to have seen a ghost then at least three people in this room should have experienced something they can't explain, and I'm not just talking about Hashim's hairstyle."

There were a few snickers and snorts from around the room. Hashim stared stonily at his desk, muttering under his breath.

"Now, as you have wasted all of my lesson with your appalling behaviour, you will get homework instead, to be completed tonight and presented in class tomorrow. Failure to comply will result in a visit to the head."

"Sir!" Hashim protested instantly, but Mr Bacon spoke over him.

"You will work in groups, to be chosen by me. You will all pick one scene from *Hamlet* and rewrite it in contemporary language."

Jay groaned along with the rest of the class. "You will bring it in for discussion in tomorrow's lesson where *each* group member will take part in reading the scene and talking about how you decided to approach the task." Mr Bacon hesitated for a second as he glanced round the room. "Kelly, Jay, Hashim... Bethan and Emily. You're one group."

"I'm not going near *her*, no way!" Kelly spat the words out and crossed her arms, nodding sharply at Emily.

Mr Bacon struggled to look Kelly in the eye; it wasn't just the kids who found her intimidating. Kelly wasn't particularly tall or big – she was pretty average for a fifteen-year-old – but those steely eyes had the power to cut you down with a glance, even if you were a grown man and a teacher.

"She's filthy, sir," Kelly sneered. "And no way am I catching anything off her!"

"I'm not arguing, Kelly," said Mr Bacon firmly. "You do this or you do detention for the rest this week and all of next."

Kelly arched a thin eyebrow. "I won't do it."

Mr Bacon took a breath. "Then I'll have to call your

father, won't I?" The class hissed as if he had somehow just broken all the rules of engagement. Kelly had seen more than most in her short life. It was no secret that her brother was in jail for attempted murder, and her father used his fists first and asked questions later. There was a lot to pity poor Kelly King for, but nobody dared to feel sorry for her or she'd have something to say about it.

Mr Bacon knew just as well as they did what kind of a man Kelly's dad was. Any punishment he dished out would be a thousand times worse than detention. Kelly's stony glare did not waver, but the muscles in her throat contracted as she swallowed.

"You will work in the group I have set for you, Kelly, and you will bring in the project tomorrow. Perhaps if you get to know some of the people you treat so badly, you might feel differently about the way you talk to them. Agreed?"

Kelly nodded stiffly, and mumbled an insult under her breath that Mr Bacon chose not to hear. The bell sounded and was drowned out by the scrape of chairs being pushed back.

"Hold on, hold on… you can go when I've allocated your groups!" Jay heard Mr Bacon telling the rest of the class as he walked out. Jay stood in the corridor and waited for his heart to stop racing. Somehow he, Jay Romero, class geek, ginger bloke and all-round loser, had ended up in a group with *Kelly King*. He'd had a thing for Kelly since the first moment he'd seen her careering towards him across the playground. He had been five years old at the time and Kelly was about to knock him over in a seriously hardcore version of 'It'. She'd spent the next few years ignoring and despising him in turn, neither of which did anything to change how he felt about her.

Jay jiggled nervously as he waited for her to emerge from class, thinking, *Me and Kelly. In a group! Together!* He wondered how he was going to think about anything else.

Bethan was the next out. She saw Jay standing by the noticeboard and sighed. It could have been worse, she supposed. At least one other person in her group had a brain. It was a stupid, pointless kind of brain that was only interested in science and useless information, but at least it worked. All Kelly cared about was her hair, her fingernails and biting off everyone else's head; Hashim was only interested in football. And Emily?

Unlike most of her class, Bethan didn't hate Emily just for being Emily. But also unlike the rest of the class, Bethan was perfectly happy to be separate from the herd. She was the only one who read books for pleasure, the only one who preferred art and literature to killer-zombie computer games and boy bands. The other kids called Bethan punk or emo because of her ever-changing hair colour and preference for dressing in black. She liked to think of herself as a free spirit.

What Bethan didn't understand was why Emily didn't do something to improve her chances of survival in the school jungle. Wash her hair maybe, or wear something different occasionally. Still, if she had to work with Emily, she'd at least be nice to her.

Bethan looked at Jay. He was a little too tall and a little too thin to be good-looking, and with his red hair brushed into no particular style at all, he positively screamed geek. But still, there was something interesting about him.

Just then, Kelly marched out of the classroom, complaining loudly. Seeing Jay, she stalked over to him. As Bethan followed, she noticed a red blotch flush across Jay's nose as he drew himself up straight. He may have been a good five centimetres taller than Kelly, but she still seemed to tower over him.

"Well, there's no problem, is there, Jay?" Kelly informed him. "You'll do the stupid homework, won't you? Like you always do."

Bethan chewed her lip irritably. A lot of the kids used Jay's homework service, something he'd managed to get away with for years, knocking up coursework on his PC at home, complete with the expected level of intelligence and mistakes depending on the pupil. It was probably the only reason the mob tolerated him, Bethan thought; that and his talent for getting them through a double period without having to learn anything at all. Otherwise he could easily have been a victim just like Emily. Of course Kelly would expect him to do their project; she was always looking for the easy way out. Bethan was about to say so when Jay, surprisingly, found his voice.

"Um, the thing is, Kelly," he squeaked, the pitch rising and falling like a yo-yo, "is, well, we all have to talk about it in class tomorrow, don't we? And, yeah, I *could* do it – easily. But, well, I don't want you to get into trouble with your dad."

Kelly looked sharply at Jay and for a moment he thought she might have worked out that he was just trying to find a way to spend some time almost alone with her. She pursed her lips.

"We can't go back to mine," she said finally.

"We can go to mine," Bethan put in quickly, seeing a chance to save her grades. "Dad will be at work and Mum's going out, so I should have the place to myself."

Kelly nodded reluctantly, saying nothing.

"So all we need now is…" Bethan looked round as Hashim bowled out of class with the last of the stragglers. "… him."

"I'm not coming," Hashim said simply, grinning as he walked backwards down the corridor away from them.

"But you have to…" Bethan began.

"Well, sorry, love, I'm not. I've got a match, like *now*. You do it, and I'll turn up and look handsome tomorrow, OK? Later!" He turned on his heel and sprinted round the corner out of sight.

Bethan supposed no one could argue with that. Hashim really was gorgeous, and if he was interested in anything apart from football and his looks, she could easily have fancied him herself. But given he was really only a pretty face, his presence in the group would make no difference to the outcome.

"Well, if he's not doing it then—" Kelly began.

"Forget it," Bethan said, determined not to let the project fail completely. "We can't all bail out. Look, it won't take long. We'll pick the shortest scene we can find and be out of there in an hour, I swear."

Kelly looked sceptical, but the long, now empty corridor didn't look much better. All of her friends had already gone and these days she avoided walking home alone. Carter and his gang were still seeking revenge for what her brother Sean did to Wilson Smith. Not for the first time she mentally cursed Sean's stupidity.

It wasn't that she was scared exactly. She just had this constant feeling that someone was always waiting for her. Waiting for a moment when she was on her own. Kevin Carter was out for revenge. Carter was after her and it was only a matter of time until he got her. As Kelly watched the shadows gather at the end of the hallway, she decided that hanging out with losers was better than being alone.

"Whatever. Let's get it over with then."

Jay picked up his bag and the three of them began to trudge towards the exit.

"Um, hello?"

They turned round and saw Emily standing a little way away from them. She was easy to miss, standing under a fluorescent tube that had gone dead. In her grey and black clothes, she almost looked like a shadow. "Am I…?"

"Oh, for God's sake," Kelly growled.

"Come on, Emily," Bethan said. "I live on the estate. It's not far."

Jay, Kelly and Bethan, with Emily trailing slightly behind, walked out of school into the chill of the February afternoon. The sun was already sinking behind the towers on the Oakhill Estate and the street lights began to flicker on above their heads as they made their way towards Bethan's home.

On the playing field behind the school, Hashim raced on to the pitch to take up his key position as captain and midfield engine. The ref flipped the coin and it came up heads. Hashim always picked heads. It always came up heads. It was just another thing that fuelled his legendary status among his teammates and opponents. Hashim chose to play the first half towards the school end. It was his lucky end;

he'd never lost a game yet when he started playing that way.

It was just an ordinary afternoon, typical of Woodsville, where it got darker a little earlier than other towns. The shadows gathered just a little more densely in the corners of the estate, like groups of whispering conspirators keeping close secrets.

All over town, normal, everyday Woodsville people were doing normal, everyday things, just like Jay, Kelly, Emily, Bethan and Hashim. And yet soon, four of those five students would look back at recent events and struggle to make sense of it all.

And the fifth one?

The fifth one would be dead.

CHAP✝ER ✝WO

"Mu-um?" Bethan called as she let herself in to her flat. She was hoping her mum would already be out. Her mum and dad had to be the most average parents a girl could have and Bethan frequently wished they were more interesting or cool. But at least her mum never told her to forget about her dreams of journalism and get a job at the car plant. And her dad had never once told her that she was "*not* going out looking like that."

She cringed at the thought of her mum's dyed hair with the roots growing out, and her tops that were meant for someone at least twenty years younger and three sizes smaller. And her dad told rubbish jokes to everyone he met, even the teachers at the last parents' evening. None of the people that were waiting to come into the flat had ever met her parents before and Bethan was guiltily hoping that wouldn't change.

"Mum!" she called again, a little more sharply this time. "Are you in?" There was no reply, but somehow the flat didn't seem empty.

Bethan led the others into the living room that her mum had insisted on decorating as if it were a country cottage, complete with dark wood beams glued to the ceiling and brass horseshoes nailed to the wall. "Sit down then," she said, nodding at the dining table before Kelly King could make any comment about the decor. "Anyone want a drink?"

On her way to the kitchen, Bethan checked her parents' room just to make sure her mum wasn't asleep in there, which she sometimes was if she had a headache. The room was empty and the bed made. Bethan glanced into the bathroom, which was empty too, and even checked her own room. No one was home; the flat had been empty when she arrived. Which made sense.

Bethan set a tray of drinks in mismatched glasses down on the table. "Let's get on with it, OK?"

The four looked at each other uneasily, each thinking that they'd rather be pretty much *anywhere* else in the world than there. But that thought was the only thing they had in common.

"Right," Bethan said. Seeing that no one else was going to start, she took her copy of *Hamlet* out of her bag. "I think we should do this scene. Act one, scene four."

She waited for the others to find the page. "It's the one with the ghost in. We'll start from *Enter Ghost*, OK? Got it?"

Emily, the last to find her book, opened her copy and rubbed her palm along the crease of the spine to make the page lay flat.

Bethan looked around the table. "Well?"

"Don't ask me," Kelly said with a shrug. "I don't know what he's going on about, this Shakespeare bloke. I'm just here cos I've got to be."

"I'm with her," Jay said apologetically, risking a glance at Kelly's perfect profile.

Emily remained silent, her head tipped forward slightly so that her light brown hair hung over her face. She seemed to express similar feelings without saying a word.

"OK," Bethan said, sighing deeply. She placed her finger on the page. "This line here is easy – the one that reads, 'Look, my Lord, it comes.' We could just change that to 'Look, there's the ghost.'" She gazed round the table at three blank faces.

"I'll put that then," she said. "Unless you think it should be something different?"

Nobody protested and Bethan wrote the line down, huffing out an irritated breath as she did so.

Jay tapped the end of his pen against the table and chewed his lip. Ever since the end of school there was something he had been wondering about. He kept thinking about Emily putting her hand up in class to say she'd seen a ghost when she must have known the abuse she'd get just for talking out loud, let alone saying something so totally out there. It would have been much easier and safer to stay silent, and yet she hadn't. The only reason Jay could think of was that Emily really believed what she had said. She really thought she'd had a ghostly experience. And that interested him.

"Emily," he said, surprising everyone. "You know in class earlier – what did you mean when you said you'd seen a ghost?"

Emily glanced up briefly at Jay, before dropping her gaze and shrugging. "I don't know," she said awkwardly. "Mr Bacon asked a question. I answered it, that's all."

"You mean you really think you've seen a ghost?" Jay asked her, although he could see she was hoping he'd just shut up again.

"Don't be retarded," Kelly snorted. "She's just trying to get attention. No one would know if she was alive or dead if she didn't do mental stuff like that to get herself noticed. Stupid cow."

"Hello?" Bethan said, watching Emily wilt under Kelly's withering stare. "What about the homework?" She pointed to a line on the page. "This next bit could be, 'Oh God, please protect us. Are you a good ghost or a bad ghost?'

Which isn't very poetic. That's the trouble with modern language. It's not very poetic." Bethan looked up and saw that nobody else cared either way.

"I didn't say it to get attention," Emily said with a quiet determination that surprised Jay and even made Kelly raise her eyebrows. "And I didn't say I'd *seen* a ghost. I said I'd *heard* one. Several times. At least, sort of heard something *like* a ghost because, well, I don't know..." Emily looked earnestly at Jay. "Do all ghosts have to be *dead,* Jay?"

Kelly barked out a loud laugh. "You are so dumb," she told Emily. "Totally and utterly thick. Obviously they're dead, moron – that's why they're *ghosts*!"

"Does anyone have any ideas for the next bit?" Bethan asked the room at large. The room ignored her.

"Actually," Jay said, using the word that was generally followed by a piece of trivia he'd gleaned from somewhere, "not necessarily. Some people believe that a *living* person in extreme distress – very ill or in danger, for example – can send what's known as an 'astral projection'. Like a sort of spirit version of themselves that can travel through space and time."

"What for?" asked Kelly, for no other reason than she was enjoying the increasing levels of irritation she could sense from Bethan's end of the table. "What's wrong with a phone call?"

"Well, because usually an astral projection is supposed to happen when the person is in really big trouble, you know, like about to die…"

"Die!"

This time even Bethan looked up from her book. Emily's small face had drained of all colour, leaving it perfectly white.

"But not always," Jay added hastily, seeing that what he had said had affected Emily deeply. "Um, some Buddhists believe in astral projection as a way to travel and expand the mind. And they aren't dead at all. They're just meditating."

"Oh, *please*. You cannot take this seriously, Emily!" Kelly sneered. "The only thing you should be scared of is your own reflection. All that ghost stuff is rubbish. You do know there's no such thing as ghosts or spirit projections or whatever he's on about, don't you? Whatever noise you heard, it's not anything weird, right? It was probably just some crackhead trying to break in to nick your telly. I'd rather meet a ghost than a druggie with a knife any day of the week."

There was a moment's silence, just a second of quiet, but it was long enough for Kelly to get the feeling that something was waiting for her outside in the darkness once again, sharpening its claws. "It's just rubbish," she repeated, using the sound of her own voice to banish the familiar fear that had been following her around for as long as she could remember, but especially since Sean had gone down.

"Kelly's right," Jay said, keen to reassure Emily. "What you heard was probably just someone's TV or maybe cats fighting. Or foxes. Foxes make some really odd noises. The walls in these flats are rubbish. Sometimes I can hear every word the old man next door is saying, which is way weird cos he lives alone."

"I don't live in the flats," Emily said. "I live in one of the old houses on Old Pond Road."

"Stupid bitch," Kelly said, for no particular reason.

"Did you tell your mum about it?" Bethan asked Emily, attempting to wrap the conversation up so they could get on with the project. "What does she think it is?"

Emily looked down at the tabletop. "Mum works nights," she said. "I was alone."

"That's a bummer," Bethan said sympathetically. "My dad works nights up at the plant. Is that where your mum works? On the cars?"

Emily nodded and Bethan realised that in those two minutes she had learnt more about Emily than ever before, despite all the years they had been at school together. She didn't seem that different really, when you got to talk to her. She was all right, if a bit of a flake.

"So it's just you and your mum?" Jay asked. Emily

nodded again, her head drooping as if it were slightly too heavy for her slender neck.

"Well, loads of people have only got one parent," Kelly said. "I spend loads of nights at home on my own when my dad's out and I don't get all mental about it. You should count yourself lucky in your big posh house."

"It's not our house," Emily said. "It's rented. From the council, like your flat. It's all they had left when Mum and I moved to Woodsville. It was only supposed to be temporary. That was six years ago."

"Tell me what this noise you heard sounds like," Jay asked Emily, trying not to look at Kelly who was rolling her eyes. But he had to ask, whatever Kelly thought. She might be the most beautiful girl he had ever seen in his entire fifteen years, but Jay's admiration for Kelly wasn't completely blind. Even he could see what a cow she could be. But right now he needed to know exactly what it was that Emily thought she'd heard. It was like one of his sudoku puzzles; he wouldn't be able to let this mystery alone until he had solved it.

"Well, I don't *hear* it exactly… I kind of feel it. It's sort of like a voice…" Emily began tentatively.

"*Sort of like a voice?*" Kelly mimicked Emily's tone with cruel accuracy. "Either it is a voice or it's not a voice. And either you can hear it or you can't. God!"

"But *that's* what it is. A silent voice talking – no,

37

shouting," Emily pressed on earnestly, determined not to be intimidated by Kelly. "But… there are no words. None that I can understand anyway."

"I reckon it's a fox," said Jay thoughtfully. "The rise of the urban fox over recent years has been amazing. They are one of the few species of wild animal to truly adapt and thrive in a man-made environment."

"What do foxes even sound like anyway?" Bethan asked Jay, realising he had drawn her into his totally pointless conversation just like he did to their teachers. And then she realised that was not quite true. Now Emily was opening up, there was something about hearing her speak, finding out a little bit more about her, that made Bethan curious to know more – like the first paragraph in a good book.

"Foxes sound like babies crying sometimes," Jay said, as if he knew absolutely everything in the whole world. "And they howl and bark too of course."

"Silently?" Kelly asked sarcastically, the word transforming itself into a wide yawn. She shook her head. "This is such a waste of time."

"Well, go then," Bethan snapped.

Kelly's mind flashed on the long, deserted corridor outside Bethan's flat, and the threat of Carter waiting somewhere outside. "I'll go when I'm ready," she said.

"Then shut up and let Emily speak," Bethan said,

suddenly getting ever so tired of Kelly lounging about all over her mother's table as if she owned the place.

"Don't you tell me to—"

"That's not what it sounds like," Emily said, her fairly forceful interruption stunning even Kelly into silence. "It doesn't sound like a fox."

"Or maybe it's cats fighting?" Jay offered.

"Not that either." Emily shook her head, her palms resting flat on the table in a strangely formal pose as she looked only at Jay.

"How about an old central heating system, you know, clanking and creaking?" Jay said, picking up his pen and twirling it between his thumb and forefinger. He was starting to feel a bit uncomfortable under Emily's unblinking gaze.

"No, it's not radiators creaking," Emily insisted. "I told you, I can hear it, but... not hear it, and it's someone shouting, shouting really loudly, only I can't make out the words!" Her voice rose as she spoke and she leant forward across the table, her eyes locked on Jay. "And I feel that if I could only understand what the voice is saying then everything would be all right again. Everything would go back to normal. I'd be free of it."

The room went quiet and tense; no one was mocking Emily any more. Instead Kelly had to fight the urge to look over her shoulder and check that there wasn't some faceless ghoul staring at them all through the window because it almost felt as if they were being observed.

"You really believe that, don't you," Jay said quietly, almost in a whisper. For a second, it felt as if it were only he and Emily in the flat, the others all lost in the night. "You really are scared."

Emily shook her head. "I'm not scared," she said. "Not exactly. I mean, it is frightening, but I'm more... worried. I just need help to find out what it means..." She trailed off, sinking back into her chair as if she were suddenly very tired. She smiled faintly at Jay. "Maybe you could help me if you came to listen to whatever it is?"

Kelly's giggle deflated the tension in the room in an instant. "You fancy him, don't you? You fancy ginger spod here. *Now* I get it – all this was to get him round to yours when your mum's out. Wait until the girls at school hear about this. Unbelievable."

Jay felt heat flare up in his cheeks and he looked away from Emily's darkly intense gaze.

"No!" protested Emily. "I don't fancy *him*!"

This made Kelly laugh even harder. "Yeah, right," she said, sniggering so that her ponytail danced on her shoulders.

"Please," Emily said directly to Jay. "Please just come and see if you can hear it, and if you say it's foxes or radiators or whatever then I'll believe you. But I think when you hear it, you'll know it isn't any of those things. You'll think it's a ghost, or something like a ghost. If you're worried about what people will think, I won't say anything. I promise."

"It will be your little secret. Oh bless," Kelly sniped.

"I don't care what people think," Jay said, surprised to hear his irritation at Kelly show in his voice. "Not if it's interesting."

Jay looked at Emily. She seemed so desperate, sitting there just across the table from him. Her anxiety was so strong he could almost see it hanging around her, like a rain cloud.

"Please," Emily persisted. "You know all about this stuff, right? You can help me. I know you can."

Jay glanced sideways at Kelly's face. It was highly likely that when he said what he was about to say, she would laugh in his face and never speak to him again, but he still had to say it. He felt like he had no choice.

"We could do a paranormal investigation on your house," he said quietly to Emily. "A sort of ghost hunt."

"*We?*" Kelly spat incredulously. "Are you joking? *You* can do what you like, but no way am I spending any more time with that weirdo. I've been too long in the same room with her as it is." She shuddered theatrically.

"Well, I can't do it on my own," Jay said to Emily. "I'd need help – at least four people to make it properly scientific. One to measure any extreme temperature changes, at least two to take electromagnetic readings, because some experts believe that ghostly energy is a form of electricity and when there's one around, the reading jumps up. And I'd need one person to monitor sound-recording equipment, and maybe four digital camcorders with night vision and a timer-setting to do a good job."

He looked at the girls' questioning faces. "Because research has shown that the early stages of a ghostly manifestation are far more likely to be picked up that way. We could borrow some EMF meters from the science lab, but I've no idea how we'd get the other stuff. And even if we did get it, it's pointless without three or four people to help."

Bethan thought for a moment. When Jay came up with his crazy plan, her first instinct was to react exactly like Kelly had, and that all by itself was nearly a good enough reason for her to volunteer to help. But she had another much better one. If Jay really could do a proper fact-based investigation, and if she was there to help him, then she could write about anything that happened. She could turn it into an article, and a good one too, even if – *especially* if nothing happened. She was sure she'd be able to get the *Woodsville Gazette* to print it. They printed stories like that every week in a special section called 'Welcome to Weirdsville' which featured reports of strange occurrences that had happened to local people. It was all made-up stuff of course, a spoof that had turned into a local tradition with no shortage of people prepared to write in with their so-called "true-life experiences".

Bethan hadn't had any luck with her carefully researched and written articles on gang warfare or the library closing down, but she was certain that this could be her chance to see her name in print for the first time. Even if it was in a local tabloid that wouldn't know a real news story if the entire town was swallowed up by one. OK, it might not be the serious kind of journalism she wanted to do when she finally got out of this place, but as her mum was always saying, "from little acorns, giant oaks grow."

"I'll help you," she said, keeping her writing plans to herself for now. Jay looked surprised. "To help Emily," she added by way of explanation.

"Oh, thank you, Bethan," said Emily warmly.

Bethan shrugged. "No worries," she said a little sheepishly. "And Jay, if you need camcorders and recording equipment, what about Hashim? His family runs Sovereign Electrics in the precinct. I bet you he can get all the stuff you need."

"Hashim! Are you joking?" Kelly said. "He won't do it, not in a million years. Not if it doesn't involve a football or his adoring public. Anyway, why would he want to hang out with you lot? You make the chess club look like a good time."

"The chess club is a good—" Jay responded before he could shut his own stupid mouth. "I mean, you know chess – it's the new rock and roll."

"In which reality?" Kelly asked him.

"Interesting question…" Jay was saved from free-falling into full-on geekhood by Bethan.

"Who says Hashim won't hang out with us? You're still here apparently," she said pointedly.

"Only because I have to be," Kelly snapped back.

"Well, I keep on telling you to leave, but you still seem to be hanging around like a bad smell."

The two girls glared at each other across the table and, to everyone's surprise, Kelly did not flounce out in a fury, but instead appeared to back down.

"All I'm saying is Hashim will never do it," she said. "He never does anything he doesn't want to."

Jay knew that Kelly was right; Hashim would never do anything he didn't want to, but what Kelly hadn't considered was that Hashim might actually *want* to help. Jay thought back to that wet lunchtime when he had been sitting in the school library, struggling with a difficult sudoku puzzle. Hashim had appeared over his shoulder, as if out of nowhere.

Without saying a word, he had leant over Jay's shoulder and filled in all the missing numbers. He had done in seconds what would have taken Jay the best part of an hour to complete. Then he had clapped Jay on the shoulder and said, "And that's between us, all right, mate?" Jay had nodded dumbly and watched as Hashim picked a book about communication technology up from a shelf and slotted it into his bag without bothering to check it out with the librarian.

Jay smiled. "I'll ask him tonight," he said.

"You're having a laugh," Kelly said. "The lot of you. Completely off your heads."

"At least we're not scared," Bethan said, casually taking a sip of her now near-flat Coke.

"*I'm* not scared," said Kelly fiercely. "No way am I scared of some stupid noise that's not even a noise in her stinking house. I'm just not a total freak like the rest of you. I know that *Scooby Doo* is just a cartoon. You lot seem to think it's a documentary."

"If you're not scared then show it. Help Jay too," Bethan said reasonably.

"I'm not doing it, lamebrain." Kelly's voice rose to one level below shouting. "Because I don't want to hang out with a bunch of pathetic losers, all right? God, I can't believe Bacon put me with you lot."

"Fine," Beth said, smiling, unable to resist goading Kelly. "If that's what you want us to believe then fine. We do."

"I'm not falling for that," Kelly said, shaking her head. "I could do your stupid so-called investigation if I wanted to."

"If you say so," said Bethan.

"I could."

"Of course."

"Fine then. I will," Kelly came back, before realising what she'd said.

"Really? Oh, brilliant!" Jay said, far too enthusiastically.

There was an awkward silence during which Kelly glared at Jay as if it were entirely his fault for getting her into this, which he supposed it almost was.

"But I don't want anyone else to know I'm doing it, all right? And I'm only doing it if Hashim is. I'm not sitting around in a circle with you lot in the dark, no way." Kelly smirked triumphantly at Bethan. She clearly thought she was safe as Hashim would never in a million years agree to take part.

"Whatever you want," Jay said. "So when shall we do it? Friday would be a good time for me. All right with you, Bethan?" Bethan nodded.

"And you?" he asked Kelly timidly.

"If Hashim's there."

It was then that Jay realised he hadn't asked the most important person of all. Because, for a second, he'd completely forgotten her.

"Emily? What about you? Is Friday OK with you?"

Emily nodded. "Yes, Friday will be fine. Come after Mum's gone to work."

"Right then, I've had enough of all this for one night. I'm off," Kelly said, pushing her chair back and picking up her bag. She half smiled at Jay. "You walking back?" she asked, knowing that he lived two floors above her in the same tower.

Jay almost knocked his chair over as he leapt to his feet.

"Yeah, definitely," he said, dropping the contents of his bag on the floor as he picked it up the wrong way round. "I mean, I might as well," he added, scrambling to pick up his stuff. "I mean, yeah, I'm going your way… that general direction I mean."

"I think I'll go too, if that's OK," Emily said. "I should get home before Mum goes to work, and anyway, I'm not getting much sleep at the moment. I'm really tired."

Bethan looked sharply at Emily. "Aren't you scared to go home and be on your own, knowing what might happen?" she asked.

Emily's expression was unreadable. "It doesn't happen every night," she said. "Anyway, I haven't got any choice."

"Are you coming or what?" Kelly asked Jay as she zipped up her white parka against the cold.

"We still haven't done our project," Bethan reminded them, and for once the thought of the homework depressed her too.

"You do it," said Kelly. "You can show us what you've done in the morning."

It was more of an order than a request, but Bethan felt too tired to argue. "Fine," she said. "At least that way we won't automatically fail."

A few moments later she heard the flat door close as everyone left. Bethan held her breath for a second and listened. She could hear the *whir* of the washing machine on spin cycle in the flat downstairs, and from above came the dull *thud, thud, thud* of a garage track baseline. And she could just make out the ticking of her mother's cuckoo clock getting ready to mark the hour in the hallway. The sound of voices echoed along the corridor, shouting and laughing outside the flat. Bethan got up and dead-locked the front door just as her mum always told her to.

She went back into the living room and stared out of the window that overlooked the sprawling and mostly concrete Woodsville. It looked like a town made of children's building blocks, Bethan thought, identical cube laid upon identical cube, only without the cheerful colours. It was all grey. Even the trees that grew through the cracks in the concrete on at the side of the road seemed to be grey, half choked to death with pollution.

Bethan was always surprised that anything grew in the centre of Woodsville, it was so dirty and desolate. But wherever there was a patch of exposed earth, saplings seemed to spring up briefly before being vandalised, cut back by the council or just dying when their roots hit something impenetrable. The only place trees and plants had any real chance of survival was in the park, created ten years ago when the planner began to realise that every town needed an area of green.

It was supposed to be a wide open field lined with trees and a couple of flower beds. But the trees had sprung up everywhere, turning it into more of a woodland. They grew twice as fast as you'd expect trees to grow. Bethan had read an article about it in the paper. It was something to do with Woodsville's exceptionally fertile soil and how the trees should be studied and monitored. The council had wanted to cut them down, but there had been protests from an environmentalist group, and a local TV news team had filmed it. So, for now, the trees were allowed to thicken and spread, a dark green oasis in the centre of a grey, concrete town.

Staring out of the window, Bethan pressed her forehead against the cool glass so that she could see past the reflection of her own living room and look out at the nightscape before her. Electric lights twinkled in various shades of orange and yellow across the town, blotting out any hope of stargazing. She wondered about all of the people out there in the night, all living their same lives in their identical boxes. She wondered if any of them felt as trapped and as out of place here as she did.

Sometimes, when she was alone in the flat like this, listening to everybody else's busy lives going on around her, she felt... not scared exactly, but sort of invisible. As if nobody in the whole world knew she was alive in here. And she wasn't even alone for the whole night, unlike Emily. No wonder the girl freaked out.

As Bethan drew her head back from glass, she thought she glimpsed something move in the reflected room behind her. She spun round, her heart pounding.

The room was empty. Of course it was. She'd checked the whole flat before, hadn't she? There was nobody home but her, Bethan knew that, yet still she went from room to room again, telling herself she wasn't acting like an idiot. Only last week the druggie squatters downstairs had broken into the flat down the hall, not caring that the old couple who lived there were at home. She looked behind every door in every room, without knowing what she would do if she actually found anything. But there was nothing.

Her nerves jangling, Bethan switched on the TV and turned the volume up as loudly as next door would let her get away with. She was glad no one could see her acting like such an idiot. Jumping out of her skin like some little kid who still thought there were monsters under the bed. She was hilarious, she told herself.

And then, just as she began to relax again, Bethan was

sure she saw another something, a shadowy movement outside the living-room window.

"Now you really are being stupid," she told herself sternly, getting up to draw the curtains. "You live on the twenty-third floor."

CHAP✝ER ✝HREE

"*That* girl is so up herself," Kelly said, more to herself than Jay, as they left Bethan's and walked down the corridor towards the lift. "She thinks she's so special, with her stupid hair and her perfect life."

Jay glanced over his shoulder at Emily, who was walking a careful two steps behind, obviously choosing to keep out of Kelly's way. "I don't know, she seems all right to me," he said, perhaps unwisely. "I mean, she lives on the estate same as we do. Her life can't be that perfect."

"That's your trouble, Jay," Kelly said, pressing the down button by the lift door. "You think everyone's all right. That's why no one takes you seriously. Sometimes you've got to take sides, right? And stick to them. You can't be friends with everyone. Not if you want to get anywhere."

Jay scrutinised Kelly's profile, highlighted with a halo of harsh strip lighting. "I don't want to get anywhere," he said. "I'd rather be sort of mates with everyone than hated by anyone. A quiet life's not so bad, you know."

Kelly rolled her eyes and looked Jay up and down. "Loser," she said mildly.

Jay chose to study the toes of his trainers rather than reply. He didn't quite know how to feel. On the one hand, Kelly King, the object of his hopeless crush, had just called him a loser. But on the other hand, she had walked with him all the way to the lift, talked to him and, best of all, didn't seem in any hurry to get away from him.

The lift arrived, chiming a tinny *bing!* as the door slid open. They stepped inside and Kelly pressed the G button several times in quick succession.

"I'm not bothered anyway," Kelly said to Jay, pointedly ignoring Emily. "I know your stupid 'investigation' won't happen. There's no way Hashim will have anything to do with it."

"Probably not," Jay was forced to concede as he shot another guilty look at Emily, shrinking into the furthest corner of the lift. She looked very tired, and even thinner and smaller than she normally did.

"It's practically impossible to get him off the football pitch as it is," Kelly said, still talking about Hashim. "I mean, that lot even play in the dark, don't they? Bet that's where he is now – down the park, kicking a ball around, running into trees. I wonder if they won the match."

"Of course they won the match," Jay said. "Hashim never— Oh!"

The lift shut down. Not only did it judder to a halt, but all the lights went out, leaving the three of them standing in perfect pitch-black.

"Where's the emergency light?" Kelly's voice sounded even louder than usual in the dark. "There's supposed to be an emergency light! Brilliant. This is just brilliant."

"Must be a power cut," Jay said, trying to hide the tremor in his voice. "It'll come back on in a minute."

He really hoped that's what would happen. He was well aware that at fifteen and a half it was stupid to be so afraid of the dark, but he was. He couldn't help it. When he was a kid, he'd often dreamt that he'd woken up suddenly in the middle of the night, his blood pounding in his ears, as if he were already afraid. And it would be so completely dark that he couldn't see his hand in front of his face. Panicking, he would flail around searching frantically for the light switch. But when he finally turned it on, it would still be utterly dark. And that was when he'd realise he was totally blind. He'd often woken up screaming from that one.

Trying to keep his claustrophobia in check, Jay ran his eyes around the enclosed space, looking for any tiny feature or sliver of light he could focus on, but there was nothing. He felt his chest clench into a small, tight ball of panic that began to bubble and grow. For a few fractions of a second no one spoke and all Jay could hear was the sound of his blood pounding in his ears.

Something touched his shoulder and he jumped, barely suppressing a squeak.

"Out of the way, moron," Kelly said, the routine contempt in her voice helping Jay to steady his nerves a little. "If I can find the emergency phone, I can call the engineer."

Jay focused on the comforting sound of Kelly's swearing as she moved around inside the tiny box, suspended who knew how far above the ground.

"It's bloody cold in here," Kelly went on, her voice sounding as if it were echoing off the walls of a much larger enclosure. "It's like a sodding fridge."

Kelly was right. Soon after the lift had stopped, the cold had crept in, rising from their feet up, and Jay's skin ached with goosebumps that travelled from the tips of his toes to the nape of his neck. He clutched his arms around himself, but he could not stop shuddering, just as he could not get the image from his mind of the three of them trapped in the tiny tin box, with nothing outside but the shadows and whatever might wait within.

Then the lift lurched and dropped a few centimetres, throwing Jay suddenly sideways. Trying to steady himself, he reached out, expecting to be able to brace against a metal wall, but instead he touched something so cold that it burnt the tips of his fingers, forcing him to snatch his hand away. He lurched, shoulder first, into the lift wall, experiencing briefly the same sensation of something freezing, something tangible but absent, flickering over his face and torso as he fell.

"Aaagh!" Jay couldn't stop himself crying out as his shoulder crunched against the metal. He rubbed the spot where it hurt and found that his coat was damp. Was there a leak in the lift? Water, electricity and a metal box – not a good combination.

"Kelly, find the phone, quick," Jay pleaded. Since his fall, he'd lost his sense of direction and was now uncertain where Kelly, Emily or the lift doors were.

"All right, you big gay," Kelly muttered. "God, even Emily's got more guts that you. Just chill, all right? I've lost my bearings. I thought I'd checked this wall, but I can't have." Jay held his breath as Kelly's fingers patted his chest, shoved him out of the way, then continued her search.

As he waited for Kelly to sort it out, Jay wished he'd noticed what floor they were on when the lift stopped. If they were near the ground it wouldn't seem too bad, but if they were still twenty floors up, stuck in a tin box with no power at all, well, that would be bad. That would be really bad – what kind of brakes did this thing have anyway?

"Hello?"

Jay breathed a sight of relief. Kelly had found the phone.

"Hello!" she repeated. "Nothing. I thought these things were supposed to have a back-up generator or something."

"Supposed to," Jay said, fighting the urge to panic again.

"Oh well," Kelly said with a sigh. "Nothing for it but to wait, I suppose."

Jay heard the material of her parka slide down the metal wall and a soft thud as she sat on the floor. Feeling his way along the walls in Kelly's general direction, he slid down himself, hoping he was sitting roughly next to her. He experienced a sudden urge to lean in and touch her, just to be sure that she was really there. But he knew he'd probably just get a smack in the face for trying it.

"It's really dark, isn't it?" he whispered.

"No kidding," Kelly said. "I just hope we're not here till morning. I really need a wee. Hang on… God, you are a muppet, Jay – pass me your mobile."

"I'm a muppet? Why am I a muppet?"

"Just shut up and—"

A loud creak shuddered the walls of the tiny capsule and suddenly the lights were back on. Jay jumped again as he found himself staring into Emily's dark eyes. Her face was centimetres from his, as if she had been staring at him in the darkness. It was almost as if she were about to kiss him.

"Oh!" Jay's reflexes jerked his head back, clanging it against the lift wall so that it stung hard. "Emily?"

"Jay!" Emily blinked at him as if she'd just remembered where she was.

"I'm glad that's over." Jay laughed nervously, sliding himself up the wall of the lift until he was on his feet.

"Me too," Emily said, smiling up at him as she clambered up herself. Still standing very close, he could see that she had a little colour in her cheeks now and looked much less frail. Jay worried that perhaps Kelly was right after all. Maybe Emily did like him in that way. And if she did, well, he'd be flattered and everything, but it was no good. He couldn't fancy Emily back. Not while there was even the tiniest shred of hope that Kelly might one day look at him differently. And actually, not even if there wasn't.

Remembering his damp jacket, Jay patted his palms over his body again, but it must have been his imagination, the cold or the dark – his clothes felt perfectly dry.

All on their feet again now, Jay edged a few steps away from Emily as the lift finally rumbled its way down to the ground floor. Outside in the chill night air, the three stood together for a moment.

"See you tomorrow then?" Emily said to Jay.

"Yeah," Jay said. "See you in school."

Emily hesitated, as if she wanted to say something else, but then she caught the scornful look on Kelly's face and turned on her heel, walking towards the main exit of the estate. Jay watched her go, inwardly impressed by her apparent lack of worry about the dark or being on her own. She was obviously much stronger and much more determined than he would have ever guessed from her appearance. But then he supposed she had to be, to keep coming to a place every day where all she got was hate and ridicule.

"Come on then," Kelly said, taking a few steps towards Holly Tower where they both lived. Jay hesitated.

"I thought I'd go and find Hashim," he said uncertainly, not wanting to leave Kelly.

"Oh, right," Kelly said, drawing the hood of her white parka up around her ears and glancing in the direction of home. It seemed quiet, as if everyone were indoors, but you could never be completely sure. "It's up to you," she said. "But it's probably just a waste of time."

Jay glanced at her face, half covered by shadows. There was something in the way she was standing, the way the pitch of her voice had altered just slightly, which told him she didn't want to walk back to her flat on her own.

"Actually," he improvised, "I need to get something from home first. I might as well walk back with you now."

He was rewarded with one of Kelly's genuine smiles that made him feel certain that somewhere inside there was a sweet, funny girl who wasn't half as frightening as she made out.

"If you like," she said. And Jay did like because he knew that, for whatever reason, Kelly really wanted him with her just then.

And that made him feel great.

CHAP✝ER FOUR

*J*ay's mobile phone vibrated in his pocket as headed out into the night to find Hashim. "Hello, Mum," he said as he pressed the answer button.

"Jay, where are you?" his mum asked anxiously. "It's almost nine o'clock."

"I know," Jay said. "I was doing some homework round a mate's house and I… I left my… PE bag there so I have to go back and get it. I've got games tomorrow and it's dirty, and you know Mr Lowe will freak if I don't have a clean kit. I won't be long."

"I don't like you wandering around this late, you know I don't." His mum's voice sounded unreal in Jay's ear as he trudged along the path. "Just leave it. I'll write you a note," she pressed, making Jay feel bad about his lie. He stopped and looked back up at Holly Tower, trying to work out which window his mum would be looking out of.

"I'll be half an hour," he said. "Don't worry."

He ended the call and headed across the concrete plains of Oakhill Estate. The paving was cracked and crazed, weeds and saplings shooting up wherever the concrete had crumbled away. He knew exactly where he'd find Hashim.

As he walked out of the estate and into open ground, Jay found he was looking at himself as he would appear on a movie screen, a lone figure hunched up against the cold as he made his way between the orange pools of street light. He wondered if this was some kind of weird astral projection; he could almost feel a part flying out of himself and looking back at his body, moving and walking without him in it. It was a peculiar feeling, but it wasn't the first time it had happened; sometimes, especially at night, the real world just didn't seem that real any more.

He wasn't completely mad, Jay told himself as he made his way towards the park where he knew Hashim and his mates would still be playing football after the match had ended. If the cutting-edge theories of modern physics were true then he might even be right.

His favourite theory was that this universe, the one he was walking through right now, was just one of an infinite series of parallel universes, each one basically the same, but also radically different, like each of the hundreds of flats on the estate. And that maybe other versions of him were doing almost the same thing that he was doing now, except if one version turned left instead of right, that would create another alternative universe, and every time a version of him made a different choice, another universe would split off, and so on, and so on.

If Jay properly understood a little of what he had read then all of these alternate realities existed in exactly the same place at the same time, each vibrating on a slightly different cosmic wavelength. And if that were possible, Jay thought, then it wasn't impossible that sometimes they got a little bit mixed up. Maybe sometimes everything you thought of as being real wasn't real at all, and the things you told yourself were just in your head might be true.

And that was the reason he was keen to find out what Emily's ghost really was. He knew exactly how to look for a ghost because he thought that ghosts might be real, but he didn't think they were the spirits of dead people. His own theory was that they were voices or shadows from another universe. Not that Emily's sounded like a typical ghost. Maybe the noise that Emily kept hearing was even another version of Emily that kept half slipping into the wrong reality.

But it was easier to let Kelly and the others think he believed in restless spirits than it was to explain that theory. Somehow the dead people idea seemed less wacky. They'd think Jay was a *total* nutter if he told them that he was quite sure that one day he'd turn round a corner and bump right into himself.

Jay stopped at the locked park gates and listened. Sure enough, he could hear the shouts of Hashim and his mates as they played Blackout Footy.

It had been Hashim's invention; something he'd come up with as winter shortened the daylight hours the obsessed boys had to play their favourite sport. He'd taken a football and painted it with fluorescent paint, then charged it under an electric light all day. And then, when it was dark, him and his footy mates would scale the park gates and play.

The glow of the ball would last for half an hour or so, after which the game turned into a frantic and frequently violent scrum where no one could see their opponent coming at them, let alone find the ball to kick. The unusually high number of trees that grew right where the pitch should be made very hard and unforgiving obstacles, resulting in a catalogue of injuries which all the participants wore like badges of honour. There didn't seem to be any rules, except to score as many goals and hurt as many people as possible in the process.

The park gates were locked at dusk, but the fence never kept anyone out who really wanted to get in. Jay knew that Hashim was somewhere in there among the trees, but he didn't know who else might be there too. Muggers or smackheads or worse. But he had to speak to Hashim tonight if there was any chance of getting the equipment he needed for Friday. Reminding himself of the answers that might be waiting in Emily's house, he hauled himself up and over the park railings. He took a deep breath and headed towards the sound of voices.

Jay felt the tackle before he saw the boy who hit him feet first, bringing him down hard on to the wet, muddy ground. *"Umphf!"* was the only noise he could make as all the air was knocked out of him. The boy who had brought him down ran on, shouting, "Over here, pass it over here!" to no one in particular.

"Wait!" Jay gasped. "Hey, come back a minute!"

Three more lads streaked past him so close that the wind they created ruffled his hair, the soles of their trainers only just clearing his prone form by millimetres. "Tackle him!" one hollered, his voice echoing off the bare branches of the trees.

Gingerly, Jay sat up, realising he'd wandered right into the middle of the game.

"Hashim!" he yelled, finding his voice again. "Hashim, where are you?" He felt a rush of air graze his cheek and the *thrum* of the ball as it clipped his ear. It stung.

"Deflection!" someone shouted. "Shoot! *Shoot!*" Then that someone ran right into Jay, tripping over his legs and plummeting to the ground.

"Oi!" Hashim yelled. "No tripping, we said. That's well out of order, man." He peered through the dark at the culprit, his scowl turning to a frown when he recognised Jay.

"What are you doing here?" Hashim asked, forgetting the game for a second.

"I need to talk to you," Jay began as Hashim scrambled to his feet.

"I told you, mate, I don't know anything about Shakespeare. Now seriously, get out of here if you don't want to get hurt."

"It's not about that," Jay persisted, ducking just in time to avoid a football thumping into the side of his head, anticipating its approach just in time.

Expertly chesting the ball down to his feet, Hashim's head turned in the direction of a series of shouts and yells which had erupted at one side of the park. "They've gone and scored," he said angrily. "That's your fault, that is. They never score if I'm there."

"Who has?" Jay asked him. "How do you know it's not your side who's scored? And anyway, you've got the ball!"

"There's more than one ball, Jay – keep up!" Hashim laughed at that, then held out a hand. "Get up," he said. "So what do you want? Be quick."

"Your help," Jay said, resisting the urge to rub his stinging ear.

"My help with what?" Hashim said, keeping half an ear

on the game. "Do you want coaching or something? Because I'm not being funny, mate, but I don't think you've got the legs for it."

"Hashim, over here!" someone yelled as the hub of the match stampeded closer, dark shadows and silhouettes ducking in and out of the trees, lit only by street lights and the moon. In the confusion, it was hard to tell the solid people from the shadows and the shadows from the solid people; there could have been ten people playing or fifty. Jay had no idea.

Impatient to be back in the thick of it, Hashim looked expectantly at Jay. "Spit it out, mate."

On the way over Jay had rehearsed in his mind how to get Hashim involved in his plan without putting him off straightaway. He knew Hashim would never sign up for some freak ghost hunt, not just like that, even if he was hiding a brain the size of a planet. So he appealed to the part of Hashim that the world knew best. The rebel.

"I want to nick something from school," Jay said. "And I need your help to do it."

Hashim peered at Jay for a moment then shrugged. "Cool," he said. "I'm in."

"Don't you want to know what it is?"

"Not specially," Hashim said. "Fill me in on the details tomorrow, 'K?"

"Don't tell anyone…" Jay started, but Hashim was

already gone, leading the pack of players away into the pitch-black.

The next thing Jay heard was the victorious cry of "Gooaaaaaaaaaaaaaaaal!" somewhere in the darkness. Alone, he stood on the wet grass and looked around. It was funny how, when all the players had headed towards the other end of the park, it seemed that some of them had left their shadows behind, flitting in and out of the trees.

"Trick of the light," Jay told himself, choosing to ignore the fact that there wasn't really any. Disorientated by the noise and the near dark, it took him a second to work out in which direction he needed to go. Eventually he found the gate and hauled himself over the railings, landing back on the pavement with a *thud*.

"Fix you up, mate?" A youngish man, his parka zipped up over his chin and mouth, stepped out of the bus shelter, his offer sounding more like a threat.

"Um, no thank you," Jay said. "I've got no money."

"Got a phone?" the youth asked, taking a step nearer, his hands thrust deep in his pockets. Giving the impression that he might be holding on to something in there, maybe a knife. "Gimme your phone."

"I haven't got a phone," Jay lied, eyeing the pockets anxiously. "I'm not allowed one, or a TV in my room, or to stay out past ten o'clock. It's because my parents are... um... Mormons."

"Your parents are morons?" The youth sneered. "Runs in the family. Give us your phone and your money, else I'll cut you up."

Jay got ready to dodge, but no blade appeared. "No, I said *Mormons*, from the Church of Jesus Christ of Latter-day Saints founded by Joseph Smith Junior in the nineteenth century," he explained, wondering why he was trying to bamboozle his assailant with useless facts, instead of coming up with another more effective plan.

"I don't care if you're the Pope, mate, I want your cash now." The kid removed his hand from his pocket and a glint of metal showed this was no bluff.

Jay came up with another plan. Run.

"Gotta go, my mum's expecting me. Bye!" Jay turned on his heel and ran as fast as he could, praying with all his heart that the dealer-slash-mugger-slash-slasher was too out of it to be able to follow him. Pounding across the road and up a side street, he'd turned four corners before he realised that he had no idea where he'd been running to. But no one had followed him and that was the main thing.

"My mum's waiting for me?" Jay wheezed to himself as he sat on a garden wall to catch his breath. "My *mum's* waiting for me? If that's my best get-out-of-trouble line, I am *never* going to pull Kelly King."

Jay checked his watch. It felt like he'd been out for nearly half an hour, but barely ten minutes had passed since he'd gone to look for Hashim. It must be that adrenalin thing he'd read about on the internet. When you were really scared or your life was in danger, your brain slowed everything right down to give you time to think and react. Which still didn't explain why he'd told a potentially murderous thief that his mummy was waiting for him. Still, that didn't matter now. The main thing was that he had Hashim on the team, even if Hashim didn't exactly know it yet. That gave Jay a sense of satisfaction, as if he'd found the missing piece of a complex puzzle. Even if he didn't quite know how it was all going to fit together yet, or what might happen when he did.

Taking a breath and a moment to work out where he was, Jay began to walk back home. He had a feeling that the next few days were going to be interesting.

CHAP✝ER FIVE

"*K*elly?" Jay called as she slouched through the school gates a few steps ahead of him with a group of her friends. "Hey, Kelly!"

Kelly did her best to ignore him, but Jay was persistent, jogging to catch up and falling into step at her side.

"Hashim's in," he grinned at her.

"In what?" Lauren Brinks asked. "The nick?"

"In my dreams," Kenisha Jones sighed.

The girls giggled, but Kelly stopped dead, glaring at Jay. It was clear that the only thing she wanted Jay to do right then was to shut up and get lost, but Jay couldn't stop himself.

"In on the project... you know, the one Bacon set us?" he babbled nervously, fully aware that the hard-faced Kelly who hung with her cronies wasn't nearly the same girl as the one who'd almost asked him to walk her home last night. This Kelly had no inner vulnerability, no secret softness. This Kelly would kill him dead with a single look if she thought her friends might find out she had even a passing interest in something as geeky as a ghost hunt.

"Do I look like I give a toss if you and that loser are in on anything?" Kelly asked slowly and pointedly, arching one razor-sharp brow.

"No… I just thought—"

"Then don't hassle me, right?" Kelly turned away. "Do one, geek."

"So we'll talk later then?" Jay called after her. She didn't give him a backward glance.

Jay sighed. It was hard being in love with the girl least likely to ever love you back in the entire universe. Universes, if you counted all the parallel ones that Jay was certain existed. Still, he'd seen something in Kelly last night; something that wasn't harsh and scary and mean. And even if they didn't find a ghost, which Jay was fairly sure they wouldn't, perhaps he'd find something even rarer and less believable; maybe he'd find the part of Kelly King that could like him back. All he needed was a reason for them to spend more time together, and right now investigating Emily's house was that reason.

Looking across the playground he could see Bethan reading. Probably the notes on their group project that she'd done more or less single-handed, he realised. Really he should go and see if she needed any help before their English class in second period. A very small part of him was feeling guilty that Bethan had done most of the work on her own. But it was a *very* small part, so when he saw Hashim sauntering in, perilously close to the registration bell, he made a beeline for him instead.

"Hashim," Jay called. "Can we talk about… you know, that *project*." Jay winked. At least he tried; it was really more of a blink.

"Oh, yeah, the stuff you want to nick," Hashim said, way too loud for Jay's liking.

"Shhh… don't tell everyone!" Jay looked alarmed.

Hashim laughed and lightly thumped him on the shoulder. "Relax, mate, we're lifting a bit of equipment from school, not robbing a bank. Probably no one'll even notice it's gone. What do you want again?"

"Well, the thing is, can I talk to you alone?" Jay asked darkly, leaning closer to the other boy.

Hashim looked around the now near empty playground. "I think you'll find you are," he said. "And no offence, but respect my personal space, yeah?"

He was right. The playground was all but empty, but Jay still nudged him over to the spot behind the wheely bins where the smokers failed to hide their habit from the rest of the school.

"So?" Hashim said as if he were a little afraid that Jay's

lack of cool would rub off on him if they spent too long together.

"So what I asked you last night, that's true; I do need to get some stuff from the school, from the science block. I need some EMF meters and a few other bits. But that's not all. I need some other stuff too."

"What other stuff, man?" Hashim asked with an amused smile. "A Bunsen burner and a couple of test tubes?"

"Four HD digital camcorders with night vision and a timer, two digital audio recording devices and at least one TV or monitor to hook up to the camcorders, preferably wireless," Jay told him.

"What?" Hashim laughed. "I'm not turning over Dixons, mate. You don't get youth trials at the major clubs if you've got a criminal record."

"Yes, but you don't have to. Your parents run a shop, don't they? In the precinct?"

Hashim's smile faded and he folded his arms. "I'm not robbing my parents either. You asked me to get some stuff out of school for you. I'll do that – it's a laugh and anything that might piss off the school's fine by me. But what do you think I am, Jay? If you want some low-life criminal then you need to get one of the gangs to help you. But not me. I got a future and I got a family, and you're well out of order."

"No! I know and I'm not asking you to steal from your

family," protested Jay. "I thought you could just borrow them secretly, and then we could put them back again afterwards."

"After what?" Hashim asked him. "What are you planning to do with hundreds of quids worth of gear anyway?"

Jay paused. "I'm going to see if Emily Night's house is haunted," he said eventually because he couldn't think of any other way to put it. "Bethan and Kelly are in on it, and with you on board I think we can really make it a proper investigation."

Hashim stared at him. "Me on board?" he asked. "What are you talking about?"

Jay took a breath. "Last night round Bethan's, when we were supposed to be doing that project, Emily told us about her ghost. She said she thought her house was haunted. And she wasn't joking – she looked really scared and worried. So I said that I'd do an investigation, you know, like a ghost hunt. Check out her house – more for a laugh and to help her calm down than anything, because I don't really believe in ghosts. But anyway, to do it properly I need the EMF readers, the camcorders, the monitors..."

He stopped as Hashim doubled up, helpless with laughter.

"That's funny, that's really funny. You thought you'd get me in on your mental-like geek games?" he said. Then he suddenly stopped laughing, as if he'd just remembered something and straightened up, all trace of humour gone from his face. "I don't think so."

The registration bell sounded and Jay tensed automatically, but Hashim didn't seem in any hurry to get to class.

"Look, I'll help you get the EMF readers," Hashim told him, "because I don't go back on my word. But, mate, my parents would never let me out of the house again if they knew I'd taken stock from the shop for you to muck around with. Even if I could get it, we don't have that much stuff right now – I'd probably only be able to get you two camcorders and one monitor at that. And besides, how were you planning to carry it all around? On the bus?"

"Well, I…" Jay hadn't thought of that. "What about your brother? He's got a car, hasn't he?"

"Farid?" Hashim laughed again. "I can't exactly see my big brother helping me do over our parents."

Jay wracked his brains. "You could say it was for a science project for school, then your parents wouldn't mind and Farid would have to help you."

"I could, but I'm not going to because I don't want to be in on your little ghost hunt. It's all crap anyway, and if Kelly King has said she'll help you then you can bet your life that it's only because she's seen some way to humiliate you, or Emily, or all of you, and you just don't know it yet."

"She's doing it because I told her *you* were," Jay said, before he could stop himself.

"Kelly King wanted to do it because she thought I was?" Hashim's demeanour changed from tense and irritated to interested in one second flat. He liked Kelly too, Jay realised with a heavy heart. Of course he did. Any boy would have to be dead not to fancy Kelly with her flashing eyes and shiny curls.

So Kelly would only do it if Hashim did, and Hashim was only interested if Kelly was involved. As the only way Jay could think of spending any time at all with Kelly outside of school and away from her mob was during a ghost hunt at Emily's house, there was nothing else for it.

"I think she likes you," Jay lied with a shrug.

"I suppose that science project idea *could* work..." began Hashim thoughtfully.

"And anyway, you'd look pretty cool setting up all the equipment, measuring the fluctuations in temperature and electromagnetic fields. I don't think I could do all of that technical stuff properly without you. I bet you'd be really good at it."

"All night with Kelly King..." Hashim almost cracked a smile.

"Look, Hashim," Jay was keen to stop him thinking about Kelly. "You and I both know you've got brains, even if you always hide them. You're essential. If you're in on this then it will be a real scientific experiment. Without you, it's just going to be a girly sleepover at Emily Night's."

"A girly sleepover? All right then, count me in." Hashim made up his mind. "Meet me here after school and we'll get the EMF readers."

"Right after school? Shouldn't we wait until school is shut or something?" Jay asked anxiously. But before Hashim could answer they were interrupted.

"You boys! What do you think this is, a holiday camp?" Bacon bellowed across the concrete. "Head's office. NOW!"

"Just be here, Jay-boy," Hashim said, before waving cheerily at Bacon. "Nice morning for it, isn't it, sir?"

CHAP✝ER SIX

Jay held his breath and listened to the beat of his heart as he waited for Hashim after classes ended for the day. The bell had rung twenty minutes ago and Hashim had still not turned up. Jay stood watching his fellow pupils bundle out of school, hugging himself against the cold, shifting from foot to foot until the playground was empty.

The lights were still on in the building behind him and Jay knew that there would be teachers around for at least another hour, which made the standing about in the dark a less lonely prospect, even if it made the breaking into the science labs a little trickier. He wondered if Hashim had changed his mind or forgotten. Still, as Jay didn't have anything more exciting to do except for his own geography and two other people's maths homework, he waited.

Woodsville after dark was never the friendliest place to

be. In the town centre, the bars and nightclubs buzzed from Thursday to Sunday. The streets swarmed with girls dressed for summer, no matter what the season, and boys wearing too much aftershave, full of too much booze. They mingled and collided with each other like planets until something or someone invariably kicked off. Jay's dad said they should give the High Street a Government health warning at the weekends. But it wasn't just the drunks or the gangs; there was something else about Woodsville at night, something edgy and uncomfortable.

Even here behind the wheely bins, only a few metres from where the school still blazed with light and was full of people, Jay again got that feeling of being watched. It was as if he were watching himself being watched by some unknown menace that was slowly gathering in the shadows, waiting for… *something* to trigger its final pounce.

Jay had told Hashim that he didn't believe in ghosts, but alone in the dark anything seemed possible. The sense that he was just out of reach of something very bad, something evil, grew stronger. Surely there would come a time when it would be able to stretch out and…

Jay screeched as a hand emerged from the shadows and clamped on his shoulder.

"You girl!" Hashim chuckled. "Did I scare you, Jaysey? Did I?"

"You surprised me," Jay said, composing himself and only too aware that he had in fact screamed like a girl. This was no good. If he was going to have any chance with Kelly over Hashim, he'd have to be swifter with the tough and witty one-liners, and stop the shrieking.

"Yeah, I noticed – you're white as a sheet!" Hashim grinned. "Anyway, you ready or what?"

"Where have you *been*?" Jay asked, wishing he didn't sound quite so much like his mother when he got back from school later than expected.

"Detention!" Hashim shrugged. "Relax, Jay. It's better now anyway. I got a good look round and most of the teachers have gone. Bacon's still in the staffroom making eyes at Miss Riley and the head's still in his office, but that's it. The coast is clear. We need to get in and out before they switch on the alarm system and lock up."

"Don't forget the CCTV," Jay said. "I brought this for disguise." He produced a blue and red balaclava that his mum had knitted in the Woodsville United team colours.

"That'd get you nicked any day of the week," Hashim laughed. "The CCTV isn't a problem – it's only at the main entrance and in the corridors leading up to the ICT room. No one gives a toss about the science lab; they don't figure there's anyone mental enough to want to rob from there. We'll go in through the fire exit by the main hall. I just opened it on my way here. Then we can slope round the back past the art department. That way we'll stay well clear of the cameras. Let's go."

"What if we're caught…?" Jay began to have second thoughts about the whole plan. Apart from his illegal homework racket and regular lesson distraction, he wasn't exactly a budding criminal. He preferred to keep his head down, get on with everyone, to conform. All that would change if he got caught breaking and entering his own school. "Shouldn't we have a back-up story? Like we fell asleep in class, or we forgot something important, or we smelt smoke, or…"

"Don't be an idiot," Hashim shut him up. "We're not going to get caught. I never get caught."

Gulping a little, Jay followed Hashim around the outskirts of the building, staying low and close to the wall, just as the other boy did. He felt like a cross between a ninja and an SAS operative. Hashim slowed down as they approached the fire exit.

"Damn, someone's shut it," he hissed.

"Oh. Er. Oh well, let's go home then…" Jay relaxed a little.

"No, wait." Hashim pointed. "Look, that window's not closed properly. The latch isn't down. You're skinny. You squeeze through it, then you can creep round and open the door for me, yeah?"

"Me?" Jay was appalled. "But what if I knock something

off the windowsill, or disturb a cleaner, or trip an infrared light…"

"The cleaners only come in every other day since the cut-backs," Hashim said. "Today is an off day, and it's the girls' changing rooms. No one's in there now."

"The girls' changing rooms!" Jay looked on in horror as Hashim prised open the narrow, frosted glass window and nodded at him.

"Come on, I'll give you a leg-up."

For a second, as Jay teetered between the outside world and the mysteries of the girls' changing rooms, he wondered exactly how he had ended up here. The windowsill bit hard into his abdomen, but then Hashim gave him a shove and before he knew it, he'd slid awkwardly through and landed with a bump on the floor, still damp from post-PE showers. Clenching his fists and keeping his eyes down as he passed the empty shower block, he headed for the exit. Glancing quickly either way down the corridor, he raced down it several metres, before realising that he was heading in completely the wrong direction and racing back towards where Hashim would be waiting. Jay's heart was hammering against his ribs as he finally opened the fire escape door, although he wasn't sure if it was the dark, the adrenalin or the thought of being caught in the girls' changing room that scared him the most.

"You took your time." Hashim's amused voice echoed

round the corridor. "What were you doing in there? Trying on gym knickers?"

"No!" Jay felt his cheeks grow hot in the gloom. "Come on, we haven't got time to hang around."

"This way." Hashim led him to the science lab, avoiding the main corridors and any places where a stray teacher might still be lurking.

While Hashim sauntered along almost casually, Jay pressed his back against the wall, creeping along, peering round corners, ears pricked for any sound he might hear over the chattering of his teeth.

"You're hilarious, man," Hashim told him, hands in his pockets. "All that Mission Impossible stuff isn't going to stop us getting caught. Be cool, OK?"

"I don't get it. Outside you were doing all this too!" Jay protested.

"I was messing with you." Hashim shook his head. "Man, no wonder you were suckered in by mad Emily's ghost story. You'll believe anything. A paranormal investigator is supposed to be a sceptic, yeah? Try looking it up in the dictionary."

"I am a sceptic. It's just there are more things in heaven and earth…" Jay broke off, trying to remember where he'd read that phrase.

Hashim shrugged. "Let's get the gear and go. We might have to make a run for it when we get outside again. Got it?"

"Got it," said Jay miserably, belatedly wondering why he hadn't just asked the head of science, Mr Prunty, if he could borrow the EMF readers. As a founding member of the Woodsville UFO Society, Jay was fairly sure that he'd have agreed.

Most of the valuable science equipment was locked away in a stockroom, but Jay knew Mr Prunty kept the key in his unlocked desk drawer. Prunty had put it there right in front of Jay's eyes, clearly never thinking that the boy would ever use that knowledge to come and turn the place over.

Hashim was impressed. "You've been casing the joint," he nodded in approval.

"Well, not exactly…" Jay began to explain, but then decided he liked that Hashim thought he was at least a bit cool, so he just shut up and unlocked the stockroom door, switching on the interior light at the same time.

It didn't take long to find what they were after – everything was stacked and labelled alphabetically. Jay tucked four EMF meters into his rucksack.

"Anything else you need to catch a ghost?" Hashim asked as he scanned the shelves. "Hydrochloric acid? Particle accelerator?"

"There's a particle—? Oh, you're joking again," Jay sighed. "Very funny."

"As if there'd be a particle accelerator in the school

stock— What was *that*?" A sudden, soft noise in the room outside wiped the grin off Hashim's face.

The boys froze as they both heard it again. Hashim put a finger to his lips and peered through the crack in the door, into the darkness of the lab. He frowned and shook his head, unable to see anything or anyone, but the noise continued – a scratching sound, like fingernails on a blackboard.

"A mouse maybe?" Jay whispered.

Nudging past Jay, Hashim very slowly opened the door a little wider so he could get a better look at the room beyond. It seemed completely empty. "Mice or heating pipes, there's nothing there to bother us. Come on, let's get out of here."

Just as he turned to pick up his backpack, the stockroom door slammed shut behind him with an ear-splitting crash, and the tiny room plunged into blackness.

"Not again," Jay moaned under his breath, feeling the same sense of panic and claustrophobia he'd felt in the lift at Bethan's. He reached out to grasp the edge of one of the shelves on his left so that at least he had a sense of something solid in the dark, but it wasn't where it had been the second before the lights cut out. Everything had shifted just a little, forcing him to grope around to find something to hold on to. When his hand landed on Hashim's arm, he was surprised the other boy didn't tell him to get off at once.

"Draught probably," Hashim said, but his voice didn't

sound quite as confident as it had been. Jay felt him move away and guessed that he was feeling for the door handle. When one more second of silence passed than he could cope with, Jay spoke, unable to keep the panic out of his voice.

"What is it? Is it locked? Are we stuck in here?"

"It's the dark." Hashim sounded edgy. "I can't find the… wait… got it." To Jay's immense relief, the door opened, letting in enough half-light to make sense of the room again. Carefully, Hashim emerged from the stockroom and looked around.

"Definitely no one here," he said, relief in his laugh. "Maybe the lights in the school are on a timer or something, so they all go off at a certain time. God, if we get this spooked by a mouse and a bit of wind, what'll we be like on a proper ghost hunt? Come on, let's—"

Hashim froze and stared into the darkest corner of the room. Jay followed his gaze, but he could see nothing.

"What? What is it?"

"It's nothing," Hashim said steadily, his wide eyes not moving from the spot they were fixed on as he backed towards the exit. "Let's just get out of here. Now."

Moments later they emerged from the fire exit and into the bitingly cold night.

"Come on!" Hashim called as he pelted across the field towards the school fence. Jay struggled to keep up, wondering why now, when it was pretty certain no one was going to discover them, that Hashim was so keen to be as far away from the scene of the crime as possible. By the time Hashim hauled him over the perimeter fence, Jay's lungs were burning and he felt dizzy. He collapsed on to the ground to catch his breath.

"What were we running away from?" he asked Hashim in gasps as he lay on the cold, wet verge. Hashim, who hadn't even broken a sweat, shook his head. "Oh, come on. What did you see in there?"

"Nothing." Hashim looked at his trainers. "I didn't see anything, OK? I just wanted to get out of there before they set the alarms."

"You didn't see anything?" Jay repeated. "I saw you staring—"

"I told you, I saw nothing, didn't I?" Hashim shouted. "Leave it!"

"OK, OK…" Jay clambered up off the grass and the pair walked in silence until they came to the crossroads.

"We're meeting tomorrow lunchtime in the old history block, to plan what we've got to do in the evening. Will you be able to get the equipment for Friday night?"

Hashim nodded distractedly, glancing into the dark as if he expected to find something there.

"OK, see you tomorrow then," Jay said. "And Hashim – thanks for this."

Hashim shrugged and silently disappeared in the opposite direction.

Jay watched him for a moment before turning towards the estate. Something had rattled Hashim just before they'd left the science lab, and it wasn't just the dark, Jay was sure of at least that much. But Hashim obviously didn't want to talk about it.

And if Hashim didn't want to talk about something then Jay was pretty certain he was better off not knowing either.

CHAP✝ER SEVEN

*B*ethan hovered between the dining hall, where there were chips, and the fire door that would take her to the old history block where Jay had told her to meet him and the others at lunch break. She still wasn't sure whether to get involved in Jay's stupid scheme or not. She just couldn't see how it could possibly help anyone. Bethan didn't hate Emily Night like the rest of the world seemed to, but she did think that the whole ghostly silent screaming was probably just a story to get some attention.

This must be the first time in, well, *ever* that Emily had had so many people take an interest in her. And Jay was using her weirdness to fully geek up with his stupid experiments, which wouldn't work anyway. As far as Bethan could see, all this ghost hunt would achieve was to make Emily seem even stranger and out of it than she already was, and that was the last thing the poor girl needed. She was probably much better off living under the radar like she always had, invisible to everyone.

On the other hand, Bethan realised, Jay had achieved something pretty amazing. He'd got the school's coolest girl and boy – who never hung out and didn't even like each other – to agree to spend a night in the house of the world's most uncool girl, along with the ginger geek and the class brain. Bethan still wasn't quite sure how he'd managed it, but it was pretty fascinating. Even weirder, she had this nagging feeling that the five of them had been drawn together for some other reason, something bigger than a stupid ghost hunt. Perhaps between them they would be able to change the whole social structure of the school, become friends despite everything and revolutionise the age-old system that could damn a person into social oblivion forever depending on what they were wearing and who they sat next to on the very first day of primary school. Then maybe she'd get to know Jay more and—

Then again, she was probably just being an idiot. Those thoughts were probably only going around her head because her brain could not compute the reality of her, Hashim, Kelly, Jay and Emily being in a room together voluntarily.

Besides, Bethan told herself as she finally headed for the history block, there was always her article for the *Woodsville Gazette*. That was as good a reason as any to turn up to the meeting.

Bethan's heart sank a little when she realised that Jay was sitting in the disused building on his own. It wasn't even a real building, more of a hut propped up on concrete blocks. Apparently it had been erected temporarily about a decade ago, when the main building developed a leak in the roof. But here it still was, long after the money had finally been found to make the history department habitable again, rotting away until someone could be bothered to do something about it.

Bethan shivered as she stomped through the door. Inside was cold and dirty. Ivy had pushed its way in through the window and crept over the interior walls, its thick, choking leaves making the room gloomy and damp-smelling.

"On your own then?" she sighed, by way of a greeting.

"They'll be here," said Jay. He was sitting on what had once been the teacher's desk, studying his laptop.

"You reckon?" Bethan raised an eyebrow, her optimism about social change at school more than ever seeming like the delusions of an idiot. "I nearly didn't come, so why would they?"

"You didn't? Why not?" Jay looked up and Bethan quickly looked away. No way in the world did she fancy a ginger geek like Jay Romero, but there was something about his green eyes that made it quite hard to look right into them for more than about a nanosecond. He looked at her like he might really see her, the girl she was behind the chipped, black-painted, bitten fingernails and coloured hair.

"Because I still don't get what we're doing." Bethan sounded surly, letting her hair fall over her face to hide the heat that had flushed her cheeks.

"An experiment in paranormal investigation. I thought that was obvious!" Jay said. "It says here that people who drink more than seven cups of coffee a day are five times more likely to have a paranormal experience or hear voices. Do you think that's because the coffee makes them crazy, or because it sharpens all the senses, including our sixth sense that we've all forgotten about?"

"Maybe we should ask Emily how much coffee she drinks," Bethan said, peering out of a dirty, ivy-covered window.

"Seriously, though," said Jay, "don't you ever get *déjà vu*? Or wake up in the night with your heart racing? Don't you sometimes know exactly who it is on the end of a ringing phone *before* you pick it up?"

"Always," Bethan said seriously.

"Really?" Jay asked her, his green eyes widening.

"Yeah, I've got caller ID," Bethan shot back. Jay laughed, and Bethan smiled too. He looked a whole lot less geeky when he laughed, as if all his awkward features suddenly found their rightful place on his face. He looked almost handsome.

"Bethan?" He said her name, his gaze suddenly intensifying. "Do you ever get weird feelings?" The question would have made Bethan laugh except for the fact that Jay looked so serious.

"What sort of feelings?" Bethan asked him uncomfortably, wondering where he was going with this.

"Like… like there's something—"

"Right, I'm ready." Hashim appeared in the doorway. "Do we have to synchronise watches or what?"

"And get a move on, all right?" Kelly arrived just behind, but not with Hashim. "I got places to be and people I don't want seeing me with you losers."

Bethan and Jay looked at each other, a second of silent acknowledgement passing between them, before Jay shut his laptop and got to his feet.

"Great, so the first meeting of the Woodsville Ghost Hunters' Society is now formally in session."

"Shut up, sad case," Kelly said. "I'm not in no society – I'm just here for this and I don't even really remember why. This is a one-off and if you ever mention any sort of society ever again I'm going to rip your stupid ears off, got it?"

"Same," Hashim said. He smiled and winked at Kelly, who rolled her eyes and looked the other way.

"Of course," Jay said. "I was joking. Anyway, this is the plan. We turn up at Emily's at about eight tomorrow – give her mum a chance to be well out of the house and at work. Hashim, what about the equipment?"

"Got it," Hashim nodded. "I told my mum I was taking an interest in science in case I wanted to go into medical research instead of playing football. She made my dad get us everything we need and my brother's chauffeur for the night. He is not happy about it – it's brilliant!"

"Great, so you and me can set that up first, and..." Jay looked at the girls and trailed off. He didn't like to be sexist, but something told him the girls wouldn't know the difference between the USB cable and the power lead.

"I read that if you're doing a proper ghost hunt," Bethan chipped in, "you need to check the building first for any hidden tricks, like a way to make furniture move or make knocking sounds. Me and Kelly could do that."

"Good one," Jay smiled at Bethan again.

"Also," Bethan went on, enjoying the approval, "on that ghost-hunting programme on the telly, when they do vigils and stuff in old hotels, they put a camcorder and a motion sensor in a locked room, to see if anything moves or happens in there. I could set that up. We've got a motion sensor, haven't we? It's a basic requirement for any serious para-normal investigation."

"Right." Jay was ashamed and a bit embarrassed to admit that he hadn't thought of that. "That would be cool. But we don't have a motion sensor and I don't know where we'd get one from." He shrugged regretfully.

"Oh, I could make a motion sensor," Hashim said, grinning at Kelly. She pursed her lips and breathed out heavily through her nose in studied disinterest.

"You can?" Jay asked.

"Sure, it's a piece of cake. All you need is a couple of Wii remotes and... some photocells. A 741 op-amp, a 1K ohm resistor, an LED and... um, let's see... a 9v battery breadboard and a potentiometer. Ten kilowatts should do it."

"Er, yeah, that's what I thought you'd need," Jay said, secretly very impressed. "So you can get hold of all that stuff, can you?"

"Yeah, in any hardware shop. The remotes are motion sensors already; they'd just take a bit of adapting to make them work the way you want," Hashim said, glancing sideways at Kelly, whose expression was getting more disdainful by the second. The more you knew about stuff it seemed, the less awesome Kelly found it.

"It's not clever," Hashim added. "It's no harder than wiring a plug."

"Great – a motion sensor. That will improve the quality of the investigation." Jay grinned happily. "This is going to be really solid. I can post this on ghosthunters.com and everything."

"Only if you want to die," Kelly warned him.

"So, some basic safety stuff." Jay composed himself. "Most investigators say it's a good idea to work in pairs. Because then if you see or hear something there are two witnesses, and also in case anything happens."

"Anything like what happens?" asked Bethan.

"Well, poltergeists throw things, sometimes even people. And every now and then you hear about, um, possession."

"Yeah, but none of that is really real, is it?" Hashim laughed.

"Well, there are some cases where the evidence really is compelling," Jay told him. "Like the Enfield Poltergeist in the seventies. The girls were levitated, thrown across rooms – through walls. And a lot of it was caught on camera. I can show you the photos on the internet if you like—"

"I don't care. I'm not going to be in a pair with any of you lot," Kelly snorted. "We're not nursery kids any more. We don't need to go places in crocodiles, holding hands all the way."

"But Kelly, wouldn't you rather have a partner to work with than be on your own?" asked Jay.

"I'm telling you, I'm not going in a pair with him, her or you. I don't mind being on my own. The only thing that frightens me about Emily Night's house is getting fleas."

"Fine, you can be on your own then," Bethan snapped at her. "No one wants to sit in the dark with you either."

"Well…" Jay began.

"I do…" Hashim said at the same time.

"Seriously, Kelly, are you sure that's cool?" Jay said gently.

"Yes," said Kelly irritably. "God, stop being such a muppet, Jay! It's an empty house, in a much nicer part of town than you and me live in. My brother's inside for attempted murder; do you really think I'm scared of a ghost that doesn't even exist? I'm more scared to step outside my own front door!"

"*Are* you?" Jay asked, concerned.

"No, I'm just saying…" Kelly trailed off, looking uneasy.

"OK," continued Jay. "I think we should start the actual investigation at around ten, and really we want to keep it going all night…"

"All night alone together, hey, Kel?" Hashim winked at Kelly, then blushed ridiculously as Kelly threw him a disgusted look.

"It's Saturday the next day," Jay went on, "so no school. But do we all have cover stories for our parents?"

"Told Mum I'm sleeping over with a girl from school," Bethan said. "She's really pleased. She thinks I've actually made some proper friends. It's so sad."

"Science project," Hashim shrugged and nodded at Jay. "With you. Mum loves you because you were in the school newsletter for that space project thing you won."

"I don't need a cover story," Kelly said, not explaining that she actually preferred it when no one knew where she was.

"And my excuse is a science project too," Jay said. "So we're all sorted. I think that's it."

"Hang on a minute," Bethan said. "Haven't you forgotten something?"

"Um… EMFs, camcorder, motion sensor, tape recorder… Nope, I don't think so."

"What about Emily?" Bethan asked him.

"I'm here." Everyone turned to find Emily standing at the back of the room.

"Emily, sorry, when did you turn up?" Jay said. "I hadn't forgotten you were coming of course – it's just I didn't see you."

"Well, you all seemed so busy. I was just waiting…"

"Did you hear the plans then, to get to yours for eight? We'll set up the equipment and start the investigation around ten. Are you sure that your mum won't be there?"

Emily nodded, drawing a little closer to the group. "I'm sure," she said. "She won't be there."

"Great – we'll see you tomorrow night then," Jay said.

Emily nodded and looked around at everyone. "Thank

you," she said in a small, light voice, barely more than a whisper. "Thank you for believing me. Thank you for coming."

"Believing? Hah!" Kelly snorted, slipping off her desk. "That's it, I'm off."

"Double maths?" Jay asked her. "I could walk with you…"

"No." Kelly looked at him as if he were mad. "I'm going home. I've had enough of school today."

"Yeah, me too," Hashim said, following Kelly out of the gloomy hut.

Finally Jay, Bethan and Emily were left standing in a triangle, looking at each other.

"This is going to be so cool," Jay said.

"It's going to be so weird," Bethan replied.

"But it will help, won't it?" Emily asked them. "It will make everything OK again?"

"Course it will," Jay said because he could see that Emily needed to believe that. And anyway, sometimes just believing in something was halfway to making it real.

CHAP✝ER EIGH✝

"*T*his is where your so-called science project is happening?" Farid asked Hashim as they pulled up outside Emily Night's house. "Looks a bit grim."

Emily's house was one of the few that had been part of the original Woodsville when it was still a village. It had been built on the edge of a vast forest that had covered most of where the town now stood. It was old, one of six thin terraced townhouses that seemed to huddle together for warmth. It had once been painted cream, but the main road that now ran directly outside the house meant that the exterior was black with exhaust fumes, except for where the dirty paint had flaked away like scabs, revealing the raw, flesh-pink bricks underneath.

Hashim peered out of the passenger window of the red Honda Civic – his eighteen-year-old brother's pride and joy – and felt his mouth go dry. He'd told a lot of lies to get to Emily's house tonight; he'd told his family he was doing a science project and let Jay think he was only in on the whole thing because he fancied Kelly King. But he hadn't told anybody the real reason why he had agreed to come on the ghost watch. He hoped that tonight he might finally find something out about himself. About whether he truly could see ghosts.

Farid nudged Hashim. "What are you *really* up to, bruv?"

"I'm *really* doing a science project, it's a group thing," Hashim told him. "This is where one of the kids lives. We're all meeting here."

"Any of these kids fit girls?" asked Farid.

Hashim smiled and shrugged. "Maybe."

"That's more like it. I didn't think you'd be getting all excited over science unless there was a really good reason," Farid chuckled. "Let's get this stuff dumped then. I got places to be other than babysitting you."

Farid climbed out of the car, but Hashim stayed where he was, his seat belt still attached as he looked up at the house again. Even though it looked the same as all the other houses on the street, for some reason it was the only one that made his heart pound and his palms sweat when he looked at it. It was almost as if the house was waiting for him, and it had been waiting for a very long time and had grown impatient.

Farid rapped on the passenger window. "Oi, zombie head! Are you sure this is the right address? I knocked, but I don't think anyone's in. I'm not leaving all this stuff out on the street round here. Mum'd do her nut."

Reluctantly Hashim got out of the car and, pulling himself together, went to the scruffy front door. There didn't seem to be any lights on in the house, unless Emily was somewhere at the back. He pressed the doorbell and waited. Nothing.

"She said she'd be here. Maybe she's got music on or something." Hashim looked around, shivering a bit. None of the others was here yet. Just at that moment it would have been the best feeling in the world to get back in the car with his brother and drive back home. His mum would nag for a bit about trying harder at school, and then she'd make him food and bring him drinks while he played on his PS3.

He turned back to the door. Even though the house was silent, Hashim could sense Emily was in there somewhere, waiting. Maybe she was waiting for Farid to go before she would open the door. After all, she was painfully shy and could barely talk to the rest of them, let alone strangers.

Hashim took his mobile out of his pocket and waved it at his brother. "Just leave the stuff on the step and go. I'll call the others and see where they are. We'll get it sorted."

Farid looked at his watch. Hashim knew he had a date

that he didn't want to be late for. What with the wrath of his mother versus the wrath of his very demanding girl-friend, Farid was between a rock and a hard place, and that thought cheered Hashim up quite a lot.

"All right," Farid agreed reluctantly. "But that stuff better not get damaged or nicked. If anything happens to it I will personally kill you, you get me?"

"Like you could," smiled Hashim, mustering his usual 'not bothered' shrug for his brother.

Once Farid had gone, Hashim tried the bell again. When there was still no answer, he sat down on the doorstep and slid open his phone. He realised, as he scrolled through his address book, that he didn't have Jay's number or Bethan's, but he did have Kelly's. She'd given it to him last summer, one afternoon after school, when he'd half thought about asking her out.

Then, either that night or the next, Kelly's brother was arrested and her family were all over the papers. The morning it came out, Hashim's mother thanked God that her sons never got mixed up with trash like that. Hashim never called Kelly. In fact, he'd barely spoken to her since.

Hashim sighed, digging the toe of his trainer into the dirt that had collected on the steps outside Emily's house. Maybe letting Jay think he was only doing this because he fancied Kelly wasn't that much of a lie. He did like her still, but he didn't expect any second chances. Kelly had cut off her own brother after he nearly killed that kid. He got the feeling that it took a lot to make Kelly smile these days.

His thumb was still hovering over the call button while he debated whether or not to try Kelly's number when Jay turned up.

"You've got it all. Great!" Jay said, staring at the stuff piled on the doorstep. "But why haven't you taken it inside?"

"No answer," Hashim told him, putting his phone back in his pocket. He turned around and looked at the house again, suddenly feeling uncomfortable with his back to it. Even though it was made of brick that had stood for three hundred years he felt strangely vulnerable, as if it were tilting towards him.

"That's odd." Jay carefully stepped over all the stuff on the steps and pressed the bell for a long time. "She knew when we were coming; she said it was fine. And anyway, where else would she be?"

"What are you lot doing out here?" said Kelly, crossing the road from the dark side of the street to join them.

"Emily's not answering," Jay told her.

"Oh, great," Kelly sighed. "It took me two buses to get here and I haven't got the fare home. That bitch better not have bailed or I'll…"

"You should have said," Jay began.

"I'd have given you a lift," said Hashim at the same time.

"We could have come together. Anyway, I'll lend you some money to get home," Jay finished, glancing sideways at Hashim.

Kelly ignored both of them as she looked up at the house. "That flake's probably realised what an idiot she's made of her herself and run away," she sniffed. "I could be watching *Celebrity Big Brother* now."

A dark red car pulled up at the curb and Bethan struggled out, slamming the door behind her.

The window wound down and a male voice called from the dark interior: "I thought it was a girls' sleepover?"

"God, Dad, it is!" snapped Bethan, as if the the two boys loitering on the steps were a figment of his imagination.

"Right… OK then. Call me in the morning and I'll pick you up. Have a lovely time with your friends, love. Don't stay up too late chatting."

"Yeah, yeah. Bye, Dad." Bethan turned her back on him and rolled her eyes as the car drove off.

"Yeah, bye, Daddy," Kelly repeated sarcastically. "Is Daddy going to phone you later and read you a bedtime story?"

"What are you all doing out here?" Bethan asked them, ignoring Kelly.

"There's no— Oh, hi, Emily."

They turned to see Emily standing in the doorway,

looking down at them, her pale skin luminescent in the dark that shrouded her.

"Have you been out here long?" she asked, looking puzzled.

"Ages," Kelly said, even though she had only just turned up.

"I didn't hear you knock. I thought you were late so I came to have a look. And here you all are."

"We rang the bell like a million times," Hashim said.

"But I didn't... Oh, it'll be because the meter's run out."

"The what?" Jay asked.

"The electricity meter ran out a few hours ago. Mum's at work and I haven't got any tokens. The shop's closed so no electricity."

"You are joking?" Jay ran his hands through his hair. "Emily, no electricity means no ghost hunt... I mean, investigation."

"Oh no!" Emily looked and sounded far more upset than Jay was prepared for.

"Hang on a minute," Hashim stepped in. "Have you pressed the emergency button on the meter yet?"

"The what?"

"The emergency button; it's just in case you run out and can't get any more tokens. There's usually about five or ten quid's worth of credit on there to keep you going. Where's the meter? I'll sort this." Hashim pushed past Jay, opening his phone so that the light from the screen illuminated the shadowy hallway.

"Under there," Emily said, nodding at the cupboard below the stairs.

Hashim pulled open the door. He didn't want to be rude, but the house stank of damp and the musty reek of something like rotten rubbish in the air. It almost smelt as if something had died in there.

"Here we go," he said, finding the emergency power button on the meter. "Sorted."

Suddenly the house was ablaze, bathed in yellow electric light. A TV burst into life in the front room, and somewhere at the back of the house a radio was playing at full volume.

"Blimey, no wonder you ran out of juice!" Hashim had to shout to make himself heard. "You must have everything on in the whole house."

"Mum doesn't like it to be too quiet," Emily said, hurrying into the living room where she switched off the TV.

"God, this place is rank, you dirty cow," Kelly declared, wrinkling her nose as she followed Emily. She looked around at the shabby curtains and frayed sofa with disdain. In all honesty, Kelly's own flat wasn't much better, but some savage part of her couldn't help but rip into this fragile girl who didn't seem to have an ounce of strength. Afraid of the dark; afraid of shadows; afraid of things that didn't

108

exist. She should try having a maniac like Carter after her, making his real flesh-and-blood threats.

Emily Night was pathetic, but at least when Kelly was here, no one, and that included Carter, knew where she was. Weirdly, she felt safer here in this stinking hovel than she did in her own bed.

"Right, let's get everything set up and switched on," Jay said, setting down one of the monitors that Hashim had brought. "Then we can switch these lights off and hope the emergency electric lasts for the rest of the night."

"Which is the room where you heard… *didn't* hear the scream," Bethan asked Emily, who was standing with her fingers knotted in front of her.

"My mother's room. It seemed to come from there – but then, sort of, right into my head."

"OK…" Bethan fought to curb her scepticism. "Would that be the best room to lock off, Jay?"

"Sounds like it," Jay said. "Is there a lock on the door, Emily?"

"Yes, and the key's in it."

"Good. Bethan, you set a camera up in there, and Hashim's motion-sensing device. And we need an object… something we can draw round to see if it gets moved by anything."

"What about my mum's hairbrush?" said Emily. "It's a

big old-fashioned round one. It used to be my granny's. Mum loves it."

"Why would a ghost want to move your mum's hair-brush? It's probably got nits," Kelly smirked.

Emily hesitated, irritating Kelly both by not retaliating and by looking as if she were actually considering an answer.

"Because it's old. It's probably the oldest thing in the house apart from the house itself," Emily offered. "A ghost would go for an old thing, wouldn't it?"

"Unless it was a ghost that only died last week," Hashim said, more to himself than anyone else, until he realised that everyone was listening. He grinned. "Then it would be more likely to go for a Nintendo DS or the latest copy of *Heat*."

"Well, we need something and I suppose a hairbrush is as good as anything," Jay said. "Hashim, when you finish up there, help Bethan with the camera so that it transmits wirelessly to one of the monitors, OK?"

"Yes, sir," Hashim said with exactly the same amount of respect that he would have shown Mr Bacon. Still, he got on with everything that Jay asked him to do. He even looked as though he was enjoying it.

"You coming?" Bethan asked Kelly as she headed upstairs with the one of the cameras and a tripod.

"S'pose," Kelly said, looking up the stairs with distaste. "Might not smell as much up there."

* * *

110

"Stupid thing," Bethan muttered under her breath as she tried for the third time to erect the tripod, particularly irritated because she knew that Jay didn't expect her to be able to do it. Kelly was no help; she was just looking around Emily's mother's bedroom, nosing through everything, utterly fascinated. Bethan didn't get it; it looked like any other mum's bedroom to her – but maybe that's why Kelly was so interested. Everybody knew that Kelly's mum had left home when Kelly was really little, but she never talked about it and no one – no one who valued their life anyway – ever mentioned it.

"This room's tidy," Kelly said, fingering the edge of a flowery curtain. "And clean. It doesn't smell like the rest of the house does."

"No, well, maybe Mrs Night likes to sleep in a tidy room. Who knows?" Bethan replied irritably. "Don't suppose there's any chance you could give me a hand with this?" she tried, but Kelly ignored her, opening the wardrobe instead and lifting out a floaty white dress with a pattern of red flowers – poppies – printed all over it.

"Looks like Emily's mother likes to wear bright colours. You'd think she'd get Emily to wear something a bit nicer every once in a while," Kelly said, holding the dress up against her.

"Maybe she does," Bethan sighed. "Maybe at the weekends Emily is decked out from head to foot in all the colours of the rainbow. Look, Kelly, I don't think you should be touching Mrs Night's things. She'll go mad if she finds out we've been through her stuff and we'll land Emily right in it."

"And?" Still, Kelly put the dress back and shut the wardrobe door. She went over to a cream dressing table with faded fake gold gilding along its edges and handles. Arranged neatly on it was a green glass dish with a few bits of jewellery in it, a matching perfume bottle that Kelly lifted to her nose and sniffed, and finally the hairbrush that Emily had told them about. It was larger than a modern brush, with a gilt metal handle and flat round head. The back of the brush was decorated with red and gold enamel.

"This is nice," Kelly said softly.

Bethan looked up, surprised, as Kelly gently ran the soft bristles of the brush over and over her upturned palm. "What is?" she asked.

"Mum stuff," Kelly said. "There's no mum stuff at home. No female stuff in my place at all, except in my room, and I have to keep that locked in case Dad thinks I've got anything worth selling. I mean, seriously, what are we doing here? All making a fuss over Emily Night cos she's scared of what goes bump in the dark? At least she's got a mum. If you've got that, then what's a few noises to be afraid of?"

"I know," Bethan said cautiously, very aware that Kelly

112

had never said this many words to her ever before. "You're right. I don't really know what any of us is doing here either, but, well… it's kind of interesting that we are here, don't you think? I mean, don't you wonder why?"

Kelly looked up at her and Bethan braced herself for an insult or a put-down. "I suppose it is," Kelly said thoughtfully. "Maybe we've all got reasons that aren't anything to do with Emily Night jumping at shadows."

Bethan wanted to ask Kelly what her reason was, but she held her tongue. Having an actual conversation with Kelly King felt a bit like spending time with a wild tiger; it might seem tame, but one false move and it would happily rip you to shreds.

Gently, Kelly set the brush down on a piece of A4 paper that Jay had given them and very carefully began to draw around it with a marker pen. It was the first thing that she had done to help.

"I'll leave this over here on the bedside table," Kelly said. "I don't know why, but I don't think it should be in its usual place, do you?"

"OK. But we'd better remember to put it back before Emily's mum gets in from work," Bethan said. And then, in the beat of a heart before she had time to consider what she was saying, she added, "Do you miss your mum, Kelly?"

For a second, Kelly was perfectly still and she stared at

Bethan, her grey eyes like a cat's sizing up its prey. But she didn't pounce.

"I don't know," Kelly said, bending her head over the brush as she traced its edges. "I was really little when she went. I don't know what it's like to have a mum to miss. Sometimes I think I remember something – a smell, the feeling of her, sort of soft and warm. But I don't know if that's a real memory or a dream." Kelly straightened, lifting her chin. "She can't have thought much of me anyway," she added with her usual prickle.

"Why not?" asked Bethan.

"She left me behind, didn't she," Kelly sniffed. "She left me and my brother with my dad. I don't think she could have really wanted kids."

"Perhaps she didn't have a choice," Bethan offered. "Don't you think you'd ever like to try and—"

"Ready for me to set up the motion sensor?" Hashim crashed in through the door and the slender bond of communication that had briefly passed between Kelly and Bethan was broken.

"Um, not exactly," Bethan said. "I can't work out this tripod."

"Women," Hashim laughed. "Maybe it's because you've got it upside down, love."

"I have not… oh." Bethan seethed silently as Hashim set the tripod up in five seconds flat.

"I'm off," Kelly said. "I'm not hanging around him."

"Kelly?" Bethan called after her.

She stopped in the doorway. "What?"

"Thanks for doing the hairbrush."

Kelly said nothing, heading back down the stairs.

"She really hates me," Hashim said at the space where Kelly'd been, thinking of that long-lost smile.

"She hates everyone," Bethan said. "She doesn't even seem to really like her friends, which doesn't surprise me. I wouldn't like them – they're a bunch of stupid, self-centred, shallow wannabes. But I don't think you can blame her for not liking people much. Who's she got to rely on? No mum, a dad who drinks and whacks her. A brother who's inside and... well, you must've heard Carter's gang are after her."

"What? Who's that?"

"The gang that the kid her brother stabbed was in. They reckon they're going to get her sooner or later. For revenge. For disrespecting their territory and all that rubbish. You must have heard; it's all over the estate."

Hashim had been born on the estate, but since he was five they'd lived in a four-bedroom semi in a more upmarket area of Woodsville. He knew about the problems there, but he hadn't known that Kelly was constantly under threat. No wonder she always looked so tense; Kelly wasn't the hunter – she was the prey. Carter's reputation for violence was legendary both on the estate and in school. He was one of those people who didn't care who he hurt or how badly, as long as he got what he wanted.

"Poor Kel," Hashim said. "She must be terrified."

"I know I would be. I think that's why she's here," Bethan said, thinking of what Kelly had said earlier. "Because it's not there."

Hashim nodded. "I kinda guessed it wasn't because she can't live without me, even if that's what Jay told me." He switched on the camera. "There, all done. Now we just need to turn out the lights, lock the door and wait."

They walked out on to the landing. Bethan closed the bedroom door behind her, turning the key in the lock and then slipping it into her jeans pocket.

"Well," she said as they walked down the stairs, "I don't need a sixth sense to tell me that this is going to be one of the most boring nights of my life."

CHAP✝ER NINE

*H*ashim shook himself awake for about the fourteenth time. It had been hours since they had switched off the lights. He, Jay and Emily were in the living room watching the monitors; Bethan and Kelly were in the kitchen with a camcorder, but so far nothing had happened.

For a while they had talked in whispers in the dark, although Hashim didn't really know why flicking a switch off meant that they all had to be extra quiet. Jay had asked Emily more about what she'd heard, or thought she'd heard, and if she knew anything about the history of the house, whether or not anyone had died there. But after a time Emily had stopped answering and Jay had stopped asking. There was no central heating and it had turned chilly in the draughty house, but with his coat wrapped around him and his gloves on, Hashim felt pretty cosy. All the fear and dread that he had felt outside had disappeared the moment that he stepped indoors. In fact, he felt so comfortable it was no wonder that he kept nearly drifting off to sleep.

At times like these – not times when he was sitting in the pitch black with a dreary girl and a geeky bloke trying to spot a ghost, but at times when he felt comfortable and relaxed – Hashim wondered if the fear and anxiety he felt were really just in his head after all. Which might mean that he was slowly going mad or had a brain tumour or something, both of which seemed more acceptable alternatives to the one that Hashim feared, even if he couldn't quite bring himself to admit what that was.

No, that wasn't true. Hashim knew what he was afraid of. He was afraid that if he wasn't mad, if he didn't have a brain tumour, or at the very least an overactive imagination, then the truth was that he could see ghosts. Not "orbs" or "manifestations" as Jay called them, and not only with a night-vision camera. Hashim was afraid that he could see dead people just as clearly as live ones. Actual ghosts walking around like everyone else, living and breathing. Only not living, obviously, or breathing, what with them being dead and everything.

But if that impossible thought was true, then why him and why now? The main reason that Hashim was holding out for a tumour was because it wasn't something he'd been born with; he'd only started seeing things last summer. His

Great Aunty Tahirah hadn't visited him in his cot the day after she'd been run over by a bus on Woodsville High Street. His next-door neighbour hadn't popped round two Christmases ago to inform him that he'd been flat out on his bathroom floor for nearly ten days. In fact, no dead people that he knew had ever come to visit him. But last summer he became aware of being able to see people that no one else could.

Most of the time these people ignored him. Sometimes they'd look at him, sort of mildly curious, but mainly not bothered and always at a distance. And then one had talked to him. It was the talking to him bit that Hashim really didn't get.

The first time had been during a football match. They'd been playing an off-season friendly against Eastside Comp. The game hadn't been going that well. Hashim, although better than anyone else on the pitch, hadn't been playing at his best and it seemed as if Woodsville High might draw instead of win the match. It didn't really matter, but the fact that Hashim couldn't seem to work out where to put his feet with his usual flare and confidence was driving him crazy. He had a one hundred per cent unbroken winning streak and he didn't want to lose it at a nothing game against a nowhere team. And then Hashim had become aware of a man standing on the touchline looking at him.

"If I were you, I'd stop holding the ball and pass it. Pass it to him, and then make a run up the left side; they won't be expecting that. You'll get the ball back if you pass it, you'll see."

The odd thing was that the man was several metres away and yet, when he spoke, it was like he was whispering in Hashim's ear. But it all happened so quickly that Hashim didn't have time to think; he looked in the direction that the man was pointing, picking out his teammate, and in an instant passed the ball with pinpoint precision. With the opposition's attention off him, Hashim legged it up the left flank of the field and flew into the six-yard box where, lo and behold, the ball suddenly arrived at his feet as if it had been expecting him. A quick look up to check where the goalie was then – *pow*! He scored the goal that won them the match and kept his record intact.

Afterwards Hashim had looked around for the man, but there was no sign of him.

"Great move, mate." Another boy had clapped Hashim on the shoulder as they'd walked into the changing rooms.

"Who was that bloke – did you see him? In the long dark coat with the funny hat," Hashim said. "He was coaching from the sidelines. I'm surprised he didn't get told off."

"What bloke? I didn't see anyone watching us; no one turns out for a friendly."

That was probably the first time that Hashim saw a ghost, although it had taken a few more instances for him to realise it. Like the time he saw an old lady standing in her nightie in the middle of the road, looking really confused. Hashim had been about to go and help her to the pavement when a car drove right through her. And then there was the little girl sitting on the swing in the park, as if she were waiting for someone to fetch her. Hashim might have gone to ask her if she was OK too, only *she* looked like a ghost; her lips were blue, her face as white as snow and her clothes dripping wet, as if she'd walked out of the lake. He'd stayed away from her, too afraid to know her story. It was after that he'd realised this sort of thing was happening regularly.

Most recently there had been the ghost in the science lab, the night that he and Jay had gone to borrow the EMF meters. Just before they'd left he'd seen that man again – the same man who'd coached him from the sidelines of the football game. He was standing in the corner, glaring at Hashim and Jay. He hadn't spoken; he'd only looked furious, murderous even, which made Hashim think two things. Firstly, that the man had probably been a teacher at the school, and secondly, that they really should get out of there quick-smart before anything worse happened.

Kind of mental, Hashim supposed, smiling to himself in the dark, that he would rather have a fatal disease than keep bumping into the nearly departed, but it was true. He'd rather play footy, flirt with girls, avoid homework and not think about the things he might or might not see. The longer he put off facing the truth (whatever it may be), the better in Hashim's opinion.

He had been frightened that tonight might have been the night when he found out the truth. But as he sat there on the sofa next to Jay, whose eyes were glued to the monitors, Hashim thought he knew, better than anyone, that nothing ghostly was going to happen in this house tonight.

He was wrong.

The scream ripped through the house like a tornado. Hashim was on his feet before he knew it and the girls raced in from the kitchen seconds later.

"What the hell was that?" Kelly demanded furiously, as if somehow it was Jay's fault.

"That was *not* a silent scream," Jay said as Bethan flicked on the light. They all blinked at each other with wide eyes. "Emily, is that what you heard…?"

But there was no sign of her. Emily wasn't in the room.

"I didn't hear her go out, did you?" Jay asked Hashim.

Hashim shrugged. He'd been wrapped up in his own thoughts and could have even been asleep. She might easily have left and gone to bed, and he'd never have noticed.

Then the scream came again, and this time they knew it was Emily. It was coming from upstairs.

"If she's making this up, I swear to God I'm going to…" Kelly's threat remained unsaid as she thundered up the stairs, the others close behind. Emily's bedroom was empty, but they could hear Emily sobbing somewhere.

"Emily?" Kelly yelled. She went to the wardrobe and opened it. No Emily.

"Emily, where are you?" Bethan called, walking along the hall to the bathroom. She hesitated as she approached the bath that was shrouded by a mildewed shower curtain.

"Emily?" Bethan held her breath as she yanked back the curtain. There was nothing in the tide-marked bath except for a large black spider that was desperately trying to scrabble its way out of the slippery enamel.

They all jumped as the handle began to rattle on Emily's mother's bedroom door, followed by three bangs.

"I'm here, I'm here," Emily's voice sobbed from the other side of the wood. She banged her fist against the door. "Let me out! Please!"

"What the…?" Bethan felt in her jeans pocket. Mrs Night's bedroom key was still there. She tried the door; it was definitely locked. With trembling fingers, she struggled to position the key in the lock and turn it.

"Here, let me." Hashim nudged her aside.

"It's not me!" Bethan told him furiously, satisfaction mingled with urgency as Hashim was unable to open the door either.

"Let me out!" Emily pounded the other side of the door. "Let me out!"

Bethan shoved Hashim out of the way and tried the handle again. With no warning, the key turned and the door sprang open, throwing Emily backwards on to the bed as she pulled on the handle from the other side. The others walked into the bedroom.

"It smells in here," Kelly said.

"Kelly, give it a rest," Jay said, looking at Emily, who remained cowering on the bed.

"No, I mean it smells of perfume. The perfume in that green bottle," Kelly said. "It didn't before."

"So you've got another key." Bethan folded her arms and challenged the weeping girl.

"I don't. Honestly, I haven't," Emily insisted. "I don't know how I got in here. I was downstairs with Jay and Hashim, and then... I don't know what happened. I think I must have drifted off to sleep. And the next thing I knew I was in here and I could hear her. She was screaming at me, shouting at me, but there weren't any words. I couldn't understand the words and I couldn't breathe and I couldn't get out. But she was here, I know she was. She was *here*, trying to tell me something!"

Emily grabbed hold of Jay's arm, her freezing fingers biting hard into his flesh.

"What does that mean, Jay? Does it mean that she's dead?"

"Who?" Jay asked Emily, frightened and confused by the panic in her voice. "Does it mean *who* is dead?"

"My mother, my mum – that's who was here," Emily sobbed, releasing him and wrapping her arms around her own thin frame. "She's been missing since New Year's Day. I don't know where she's gone or why, but now I think she's haunting me. So if she is, does that mean she has to be dead?"

"Your mum is missing and she has been all along?" Jay asked her.

"Yes," said Emily. "Yes, I don't know where she is."

"Right." Jay looked grim, his brain jammed with a thousand conflicting thoughts. "Well, that changes everything. I need to think. You lot go back downstairs, make Emily a cup of tea or something. I need to assess the scene."

"Need to call the men in white coats more like," Kelly muttered, but tramped off after the others back downstairs to the kitchen.

Jay stood for a minute or two alone in the bedroom. The lock on the door had not been forced. And he had seen for himself that it had definitely been locked. Emily swore blind that there was only one key, but she could have easily hidden another one that they would never know about unless they searched the whole house and her too.

There was something else though. On the bedside table Jay could see the piece of white A4 paper where Kelly had drawn the outline of the brush. But the brush was not there. Jay looked around and found it placed bristle down on the dressing table. He had no idea why he thought so, but he was certain that if he asked Emily she would tell him it was back in the place where her mother always left it. Of course, Emily could easily have moved it herself, just as she could have easily hidden a key, but Jay had been watching those monitors until the second that scream had startled them all. He hadn't seen a single movement in that room.

Feeling a sudden chill creep up his spine, Jay took the camcorder off the tripod and went downstairs.

"You're telling us that your mum's been missing for all this time and you haven't told anyone, not the police, not the school – no one?" Bethan was asking. She set a steaming hot mug of black tea in front of Emily. The only milk in the fridge had gone lumpy and sour.

"Yes, I suppose I am," Emily said, looking into the steaming mug, but not touching it.

"But why, moron?" asked Kelly. "Why keep it to yourself?"

"When I was eight, Mum got really sick. She had to go

into hospital for a few weeks and there wasn't anyone to look after me, so I got put in care. It was…" Emily trailed off, her gaze still fixed on the tea. "It was horrible. And I knew that if I told someone about Mum, that's what they'd do again. But I'm older now. I can look after myself, and besides, Mum will come back. She wouldn't just leave me, not for good. Wherever she is, she'll come back."

"But you said she's been gone for, what, six weeks?" Kelly's tone softened as she sat down at the kitchen table. It was the first time she had spoken to Emily without hatred or anger in her voice. "That's a long time. More than a holiday. Do you really think she'll come back now?"

Emily nodded. "After the hospital, she promised me she'd never leave me again. Mum never breaks her promises, not ever. If she can come back then she will. She will even if she can't."

"So where do you think she's gone?" asked Hashim. He looked nervously around the room, almost expecting to find Emily's mum looking at him from beside the fridge, or peering through the grimy kitchen window, but there was nothing.

"I don't know. I just know that one morning I woke up and something was wrong. It was so quiet. Mum always has the radio and TV on, you see; she hates quiet. I thought that maybe she'd swapped a shift at the factory and forgotten to leave me a note, so I got up, had breakfast and went out for a walk. But when I got home, she still wasn't back. There wasn't a note, and nothing left out for tea like she usually would. So I went up to her room. The bed was made; all of her things – her clothes and make-up – they were all there, and Mum never goes anywhere without her make-up. She always likes to look nice. I sat up and waited for her to come home, but she didn't. School started again, but I still heard nothing."

Emily paused, gulping a little. "And there's been nothing since, except sometimes I go to sleep in my bed and I wake up in hers, and there's screaming and shouting inside my head, and I think it must be her, trying to tell me something. Something I can't understand. Is she dead, Jay? Is she? Is that what she's trying to tell me?"

"Well, she's not here now," Hashim said out loud before he could stop himself.

"We know that, moron," said Kelly. She looked at Jay. "How can you tell if her mum's dead or not?"

"I can't," Jay admitted. He looked at Emily. "I can't tell you anything until I've had a chance to look at the camcorder, see if I missed anything on the monitors. All I can tell you is that there was nothing on the screen before you started screaming. The motion detector didn't go off and, well, Emily – you could easily have another key to that room."

128

"But I don't!" Emily protested. "Search me if you don't believe me!"

"OK." Kelly got up, but sat down again when Emily flinched.

"Look, I don't think your mum is dead," said Hashim.

"How come you're the expert all of a sudden?" Kelly asked him.

"Because I can't…" Hashim stopped himself. How could he tell them he didn't think Emily's mother was dead because he couldn't see her sitting at the kitchen table? "I just don't sense it, you know?"

"*Sense* it?" Kelly snorted.

"What are you on about?" Bethan asked him.

"Well, I'm just saying. Up until Emily started screaming, this house didn't feel haunted, did it? There was nothing on the readers, was there, Jay?"

"Nope." Jay shook his head. "Nothing."

"And the place is chilly, but it didn't get any colder; there were no sudden temperature drops. Like Jay-boy says, there was nothing on the monitors. Not even in the room where we found Emily. So I don't think this house is haunted by the ghost of your dead mother, otherwise it… *she* would have set something off."

"He could be right," said Jay. "Although, to be fair, everything we think we know about catching ghosts on camera is more theory than fact. But Emily, if you think your mum is talking to you, then maybe she is. You know, like the out-of-body experiences I told you about."

"So you're saying her mum's not dead, but she's in terrible trouble somewhere?" Kelly asked. "I don't know if that's any better."

"There's one thing I don't get," Bethan said suddenly. "You say your mum's been gone for weeks. Well, how do you live? Pay for the leccy? *Eat*?"

Emily looked guilty. "I've got one of Mum's credit cards, her emergency one. I found it on her dressing table. I know the pin so I get money when I want, I suppose."

"You *suppose*?" Kelly asked her.

"I mean, I do. That's what I do," said Emily.

"You have to tell someone," Bethan insisted. "What if your mum is in trouble? You have to tell the police."

"What's the point? The police won't do anything except stick her in care," Kelly said flatly. No one disagreed with her.

"Look, before anybody does anything, let me look at the tape, check the evidence," said Jay. "Once we've ruled out a ghost, then we'll think of other explanations. And in the mean time, the four of us can help Emily get by."

"What other explanations are there?" Kelly asked him.

Jay thought about his theory, about those thin walls dividing this universe from the next and the next, like layer upon layer of tissue paper stacked one on top of the other.

What if there had been a rip here, in Emily's house, in her mother's bedroom? What if her mother had somehow slipped into another universe and was trapped there? He considered trying to explain this to the others, but as he looked at them sitting there, tired and grumpy in the early morning, he thought better of it.

Something was happening; he just didn't know what it was – if it was paranormal, or a parallel universe, or a lost mother trying desperately to get to her daughter. But whatever it was, he had to find out, not just because he was interested or curious. Not just because he wanted to impress Kelly King. He wanted to find out because it felt as if it was his job.

"Thank you," Emily said suddenly. "Thank you for being here and trying to find out what's happening. You don't know what a relief it is to not be alone any more. To know there are some people who are my..." She stopped short.

"Friends," Kelly said, surprising everyone. "We're your friends. And we will help you find out what's happened to your mum. We'll sort this, I swear."

Everyone looked at Kelly, dumbstruck.

"What?" she snapped.

"Nothing," said Jay.

"Go for it," Hashim added.

"It's just that everyone's surprised to see you acting like a human being for once, instead of the Wicked Witch of the West," Bethan told Kelly frankly, testing their fledgling friendship with a suicidal disregard for her own safety.

"Yeah, well, it's just cos I know what it's like, don't I?" Kelly shrugged. "I know how it feels not to have your mum. I know I never knew mine really and, wherever she is, if she's dead or alive, she's never tried to get in touch with me. So listen, Emily, I've been a cow to you, and I'm not saying you haven't always deserved it, running around like a little mouse, scared of your own shadow. You wind me up something awful. But you need someone on your side right now and until you find out about your mum, you've got me and this lot. Hasn't she?" Kelly looked up at the others. "*Hasn't she?*"

"Er… yes," the others nodded.

"Thank you," Emily said. She looked out of the window where the dawn had begun to unfurl into a cold, grey day.

"I'm tired," she said, her voice as thin as air. "Really, really tired."

"Will you be OK on your own?" asked Bethan.

"Yes," Emily said. "I never hear it during the day. I'll be fine. I'll go out in a bit and get milk and some tokens."

"Right then," Jay said. "We'll get off. Let's meet in the old history block on Monday lunchtime. I'll report back on the camcorders, and then we'll see if we've got any other ideas."

Everyone agreed to be there.

* * *

132

Once outside, Hashim wrapped his coat around him and took a deep breath of wintry air. Suddenly he began to laugh, doubling up as he leant against the rusty iron railing outside Emily's house, gulping in freezing mouthfuls with each convulsion.

"What's so funny?" Kelly asked him.

"All of that, everything that happened in there! It was all crazy, man. Emily screaming her head off, turning up in a locked room. You turning into Mother Teresa. Us lot deciding to find out the truth like we're the Famous Five or something. It's mental."

"I'm not laughing," Kelly said. "And you'd better stop unless you want your brother to see you acting like a fool."

Hashim straightened up as his brother's car screeched to a halt at the curb.

"Can I keep this for the weekend?" Jay held up the camcorder that had been in Emily's room.

"I don't know..." Hashim looked doubtful.

"Seriously, I need it. Think of something, yeah? I'll give it back Monday."

"OK," Hashim nodded.

"Move it, loser," said Farid as he got out of the car, winking at Kelly. "Any of your friends want a lift?"

"Nope," Kelly said. "I'm walking."

"I'll go with you," Bethan offered.

"I could come with you if..." Jay began, but the girls

had already set off, giving the distinct impression that the last thing they wanted was a boy tagging along. He smiled at Farid. "Yes please, a lift would be great."

Farid sighed and tutted. "I was hoping for the pretty one."

CHAP✝ER ✝EN

Neither Bethan nor Kelly spoke for a long time as they trudged across the town back towards the estate. It was turning into a busy Saturday morning in Woodsville and the traffic roaring along the dual carriageway that cut through the centre of town would have made it difficult to hear each other anyway, but that wasn't why they were silent.

Bethan was still getting used to the idea that she *could* talk to Kelly at all, and Kelly was getting used to Bethan full stop. If anybody had asked her right at that moment, she wouldn't have said that she *liked* Bethan exactly, but last night at Emily's had changed things. Kelly had found herself opening up to Bethan, talking about things that she never discussed, not with anyone, and that had made Kelly think. She glanced sideways at the other girl, most of her face obscured by her blue tinted hair. Kelly had always thought that Bethan was properly up herself, with her stupid dyed hair and black-painted fingernails. She always looked like she thought she knew it all, always had her head stuck in some book, or was plugged into her iPod, listening to some indie band that no one had ever heard of.

Last night though, before the weirdness had kicked off, they had talked, properly talked, about something important. Kelly's friends might talk, but they never really listened. They'd just go on and on about boys and TV and clothes and gossip, each one talking over the other, trying to be the loudest, trying to be the most interesting, most outrageous, the centre of attention. Kelly knew she did it too because, unlike Bethan, the last thing she wanted was to stick out in a crowd. She wanted to be part of a group, even though she knew that these friends were really people she chose to surround herself with simply not to be alone. It was easier to protect her reputation that way. Tough girl, no nonsense. Don't mess with Kelly King if you know what's good for you.

But that didn't mean that Kelly didn't always have this constant nagging feeling somewhere in the pit of her gut that told her this wasn't her life, that girl talk and gossip and nail varnish and bitching weren't all there was, at least not for her. More was coming and she'd better be ready, like it or not. The trouble was that something about that nagging little feeling made Kelly certain that whatever was coming, it wasn't going to be good.

Pushing aside thoughts of Carter, and whatever else might out there waiting for her, Kelly almost smiled to herself as she hunched her shoulders against the biting wind, thinking how funny it was that she would much prefer to disappear into the background just like Emily Night. Funny how the grass was always greener, even when your life was about as bad as it could be. Someone else would always rather be you.

She dug her freezing fingers hard into the pockets of her parka and wondered why Bethan was interested in her, what she wanted from her. The two of them had almost nothing in common, they weren't exactly BFF material. Kelly caught the other girl's eye and smiled briefly as they walked. Maybe it was just that Bethan was lonely too. Maybe, for all her big ideas and I'm-better-than-you attitude, what she really wanted was someone who'd listen to her. Who'd care how *she* felt.

Kelly tucked her chin into her jacket, unnerved by her train of thought. She didn't like to admit that she was lonely or unhappy, even to herself. It was far easier to get by if she kept those thoughts out of her head. But it was too soon to know if Bethan could really be that kind of friend, far too soon. Every single person Kelly had ever trusted had dumped on her and she wasn't about to sign up for any more. She had to look after herself and right now she took a lot of looking after.

After twenty minutes, the girls crossed the dual carriageway, walking over the thin arc of a concrete footbridge that spanned the stream of cars with precarious grace.

Bethan looked at Kelly as she stopped at the park gates. Going through the park would save them at least twenty minutes or so off their walk. Many times, Bethan would never go near the park; around twilight or after dark it was a dangerous place and not just because Hashim and his mates would be tearing around it, playing football without looking where they were going.

But it was broad daylight now and, despite the chill of the wind, it was becoming busy with families – mums and dads pushing buggies, little kids bundled up in a million layers, chasing footballs and playing peek-a-boo behind trees. There were people in scarves and hats sitting outside the coffee kiosk, sipping lattes, even little old ladies who'd brought their stale bread to feed the ducks on the pond. That morning the park was a picture of normal town life, but when Kelly looked at the same scene, she clutched on to the iron railings as if she were about to be thrown into the lion's den.

"All right?" Bethan asked her as casually as she could. Kelly was scanning the various groups of lads that were kicking a ball around in among the trees.

"Just seeing who's about," Kelly replied casually. "Carter hangs out here sometimes and he's... well, you know he's been after me for a while. When I left last night to come to Emily's, someone had written 'you next' in marker pen on my door. Sean's been inside for months and Carter's been saying he's going to get me since way before that. If he doesn't do something soon then he's going to look soft and he can't have that. And I wanted to straighten my hair when I got in, and do my nails with this new colour I got from Boots, so it'd be a real bummer to get horribly murdered now."

Bethan attempted to return Kelly's grim smile, but her lips seemed to be frozen.

"Are you saying that even if Carter didn't want to hurt you, he has to?" Bethan asked. "Because of all that 'respect' crap?"

The look that Kelly gave her chilled Bethan to the bone. "Oh, he wants to hurt me all right," she said. "He loves to hurt people. He does what he likes on the estate. But what he loves more is power – that's why he's been waiting. He wants me jumpy and afraid. He wants me never to sleep and never to know what's round the corner. That's almost as good as hurting me to Carter."

"*Are* you scared?" Bethan asked.

"Of course I'm scared," Kelly said in rush, feeling surprised at the relief that the admission bought. "I'm terrified."

"But there must be someone who can help you. What about your dad or the police?"

Kelly's laugh was as bitter and bleak as the wind that numbed Bethan's cheeks.

"Sometimes you just have to accept – there's no one."

"Let's go round the outside," Bethan offered, stifling the chattering of her teeth. "It's a nice day for a walk."

"No, it's not." Kelly made up her mind. "Come on. Let's get it over with. He's probably not there, but if he is, it's done and if I'm dead then at least I don't have to worry about it any more."

Kelly marched into the park and Bethan followed. After a moment, she linked her arm though Kelly's, surprised that Kelly didn't shake her off.

"So what do you think about all that last night at Emily's?" Bethan asked, hoping to take Kelly's mind off things. "What do you reckon? Is she making it up?"

Kelly shrugged, her eyes scanning the people around them. "I don't know. But her mum has gone; there's no way she's making that up. That's what houses look like when there's no mum around because no one cares if it's dusty, or it smells, or if food is rotting in the cupboard. That's what mine looks like half the time. Whatever else is going on, she needs to know where her mum is, I get that. If I could find out what happened to mine, I would."

"I suppose your mum went off without telling you anything. You must hate her for that."

Kelly stopped, breaking her arm loose from Bethan's,

and scowled at her, her grey eyes narrowing so that they glinted like pieces of silver flint in the sunlight.

"Look," she said, "you and me have hung out and talked a bit, but we're not mates. You don't know anything about my mum, you don't know how I feel about her and you don't get to say stuff like that to me." Kelly turned and marched on, making Bethan run to catch up with her.

"Kelly, I'm sorry. I just meant that you don't go round babbling about ghosts and screaming your head off and turning up in locked rooms, but you've been through the same sort of thing, that's all."

"I was three!" Kelly snapped. "I didn't have any choice about what happened to me. If it happened now, maybe I would go mental like Emily, or maybe I would have packed my bags and gone with her, got away from this place. I don't know. But Emily's on her own in that house, her mum's gone and she needs our help."

Bethan shot Kelly a puzzled look. "I still don't get why you want to help Emily Night. You've got your own problems and they are a million times more real than whatever is going on with her. It can't just be because her mum's gone. There's something else, isn't there?"

Kelly shrugged. "Well, why do you want to help her?"

That made Bethan think. "I don't know. I kind of get the feeling that I... *we* have to. As if it's our job. Which is weird because I can't think of any reason that the four of us would ever do anything together normally."

"That's how I felt last night too. When we were all in that house and Emily was screaming the place down, I just felt like we had to help her. You and me and Jay, and even that idiot Hashim. Like that's sort of… real. Which is freaky cos it's about the most unreal thing I've ever done."

Hesitantly, Bethan hooked her arm through Kelly's once again as they finally emerged from the park and on to the edges of Oakhill Estate. She felt Kelly's shoulders relax, some of the tension easing from her body.

"Personally, I'll be glad when it's over and everything goes back to normal," Kelly added as they crossed the road, although that wasn't strictly true.

"If you can call being stalked by a murderous psychopath normal," Bethan said. She was relieved when Kelly laughed. "Kelly, do you ever get the feeling that *nothing* round here is really that normal?"

Kelly looked at her. "I don't know what normal is, so how would I ever know the difference?"

The two girls fell silent again as they walked into the estate between two tower blocks. They had to cross the whole of the estate which ranged over two square miles, flanked on each side by four tower blocks, to get to their homes. And at some point, they would have to split up.

Unlike the park, the place was oddly quiet for a Saturday

morning. There were no kids hanging out on the steps or in doorways; no groups of lads playing football on the square, even the towers themselves seemed subdued. Every window was firmly closed against the cold, many curtains still drawn as the occupants either slept in, or to keep the wintry sun off the telly. As they walked across the central square, their footsteps echoed off the surrounding walls, Kelly's heeled boots sharply clicking, Bethan's Converse trainers, with one loose sole, slapping against the concrete.

Bethan looked around uneasily. Something felt wrong. There was no one to be seen, but it didn't feel like they were alone.

"So, do you think Emily had another key to the bedroom then?" Kelly asked, the sound of her voice magnified in the quiet, making Bethan jump.

"It's possible," Bethan said continuing to look around her. "But even if she did, how would she have got into the room, moved the hairbrush and locked herself in without Jay seeing it on the monitor?"

"Yeah, I know he reckons he was watching them the whole time, but what if he fell asleep like Hashim, even for a minute or two? That would have been enough time."

"Well, we'll find out soon enough when Jay looks at the camcorder footage. It's got to be something like that. It can't really be a ghost, can it?" Bethan looked sideways at Kelly.

But Kelly wasn't listening. She stood stock-still, her face frozen.

"What?" Bethan asked her.

"I thought I heard footsteps."

"Yeah, ours, it's dead quiet round here for some reason."

"No, someone else's. Behind us."

"Carter?" Bethan whispered breathlessly, feeling her heart contract, sudden flashes of Sunday teatimes, and her mum fussing over tuna sandwiches. At that moment she'd have given anything to be at home.

"Just keep walking slowly," Kelly told her. "Don't look scared. Don't make any sudden movements." Her heels clicked on the concrete, Bethan's Converses slapped and flapped. After two or three steps they both heard it, another set of footsteps somewhere in the square. The girls looked around. There was still no one to be seen.

"It's the echo probably," Bethan said, nodding at the high walls that surrounded the square. "Someone's on the walkway and the echo makes it sound like it's down here."

"OK, so let's just go then," Kelly instructed, turning on her heel and hurrying towards home. A fraction after they started walking again the third set of footsteps started too, sounding louder now, as if whoever they belonged to was just a few metres behind the girls. The faster they walked, the quicker the footsteps paced behind them, seemingly drawing closer with every second.

And then Kelly felt a cold breath on the back of her neck and the touch of a hand on her shoulder. Too frightened to look and too frightened not to, she suddenly took off at speed.

"*Run!*" she yelled, grabbing Bethan's arm as she broke into a sprint, dragging the other girl behind her. The footsteps following them grew louder, drumming out a relentless, deafening rhythm, and they seemed to be all around. In front of the girls, blocking the way home with a wall of inexplicable noise, behind them, and to the right. The only place that seemed silent was a shadowy corridor that ran between two towers, covered over by the first floor walkway. It was dark – anything could be down there, and Kelly got the distinct feeling that they were being herded into a trap, but she had a split second to make a decision and, as far as she could see, there wasn't any choice.

"This way!" she shouted.

Bethan ran behind, her lungs burning for air. As they entered the corridor, it seemed as if they were surrounded by pursuers, the footsteps now sounding above and even below them.

"Look!" Kelly pointed to an open door that led into the lobby of one of the towers, although she wasn't sure which one. The main doors were supposed to be shut and locked all the time to help prevent crime, with entrance only gained by an electric answerphone installed in each flat. But this door was propped open, wedged with a brick that had probably been left there by one of the residents who'd popped out for something without a key. Either way it was a refuge. Kelly dragged Bethan into the lobby and kicked the brick away so that the door slammed shut.

For the first time in what seemed like an eternity, there was silence.

Kelly stared out of the toughened-glass door, her eyes wide and round, her shoulders heaving and heart pounding as she struggled to control her breathing, waiting for their pursuers to arrive. But there was no one. Nothing. The estate was quiet again.

"What *was* that?" she demanded eventually.

"I don't know," Bethan said, exhaling a breath that she hadn't realised she'd been holding. "It seemed like there were people, loads of people, running after us. Maybe it was just another echo. Maybe it was the sound of our feet, but sort of delayed, amplified. Maybe it had something to do with the acoustics of the building. Jay would know."

"And the breathing?" Kelly asked. "Was that to do with 'acoustics'? The sound and the *feeling* of someone's breath just on the back of your neck?"

"Seriously?" Bethan's cheeks drained of colour. "I didn't get that. Look, it's probably mass hysteria. I was reading on the internet that teenage girls are the worst for scaring themselves, and we've had a really strange night, and we know Carter's out there somewhere, and we were talking about it. It's not surprising we freaked ourselves out, and it seemed real, it felt real, but... maybe we're just a pair of mentals."

The two girls looked at each other and giggled, a sudden warm rush of relief flooding through them as they laughed.

"Oh my God, we were totally freaked out," Kelly laughed.

"We were running like we were in a horror film or something!" Bethan added. "Like there was some bloke in a mask with a chainsaw after us."

"Thank God this place is empty today – if anyone at school ever found out about this my rep would be..."

"Hide."

The smiles froze on their faces as the word formed in the air, out of nowhere or no one that they could see.

"Did you say...?" Bethan whispered. "I thought you might have..."

"No." Kelly shook her head. "We weren't being hysterical. There was something chasing us. Something we couldn't see was right behind us and it wanted us. And now it's here."

The two girls entwined fingers as they looked around at

the apparently empty foyer, decorated with graffiti and smelling of something rancid and sour.

"Wha… what do you want?" Kelly asked, her voice light and strained – barely more than a whisper.

The two girls stood perfectly still, each one afraid even to blink. And then they heard it, as clear as day: a long breath released like a sigh. And as both of them were holding their breath, they knew it hadn't come from them.

"Hide!"

The same word repeated, on a gasping rasp, long and thin and wheezing, but perfectly clear.

Then the temperature in the foyer plummeted, and when Bethan finally did breathe out, it frosted in the air. She stared at Kelly, trying to say, "What the hell do we do now?" but none of the words could find their way out of her mouth.

Kelly swallowed, lifting her chin. "Hide from what? Who are you?" she asked thin air, fighting to her keep voice steady and failing. "Are you… are you Emily's mum? Do you want to tell us something? Do you want Emily to hide?"

Bethan closed her eyes, expecting… something. Maybe a scream, like the one that Emily had described, or to see the shape of a woman materialise, or to feel an icy touch on her arm. She wasn't especially keen to experience any of those things, but as it turned out, not knowing was a more frightening prospect than knowing, so she prised her eyelids apart again and braced herself.

For several seconds, nothing happened. There was just the strongest sensation that they were not alone and the steady sound of breathing.

"Tell us what you want," Kelly demanded, her fear edged with impatience. "You can't just chase us around all freaky, nearly kill us with fear, tell us to hide and then just hang around breathing. I mean seriously, if you can do all that stuff then why can't you string an actual sentence together – is there a rule somewhere that ghosts have to be cryptic?"

"Kelly, you're arguing with a ghost," Bethan muttered under her breath. "It's hardly the right time to be discussing a dead person's etiquette."

"Well, it's getting on my nerves," Kelly grumbled. "It's like here we are, in a possible life-and-death situation, and it's being all vague and spooky…"

"I'm not sure that 'hide' is all that vague," Bethan countered. "Maybe we should, you know, hide."

"What from?" Kelly asked the air. "Should we hide from you? Tell us what you want. Do you… do you want to hurt us?"

Even as Kelly asked the question, she realised that wasn't the case. For some reason, who or whatever was with them in the foyer didn't feel like a threat any more.

The presence wasn't like someone that she knew, but like someone that she almost knew, someone who cared about her.

The breathing remained steady.

"Right, well, fine," Kelly said. "If you're just going to stand there invisibly breathing, I'm off." She headed towards the door, then froze on the spot as she heard a gasp sucked into thin air by no one at all.

"Now what? You don't want me to go out there?" Kelly asked crossly, apparently forgetting that just a few minutes ago the same entity had scared her almost to death. "Fine, if you don't want me to go then stop me, yeah? Wrestle me to the ground or… move that postbox thing in front of the door with your amazing ghost-like powers. Do something, right *now*. Otherwise, I'm outta here." Kelly marched over to the door then stopped in her tracks.

"What? What's it done?" Bethan found her voice at last.

"Get back," Kelly hissed as she ducked down, flattening herself against the wall by the foyer door. "Move," she spat at Bethan. "Get out of sight, *now.*"

Bethan found herself frozen to the spot.

"Hide!" Kelly whispered urgently.

Bethan pressed herself up against the wall of postboxes and stared at Kelly.

"*Carter.*" Kelly mouthed the word, jerking her head towards the door.

"Johnno saw her and another girl run down here less than five minutes ago," they heard a voice say, just on the other side of the door. "Said they looked like they were getting chased, running for their lives. Wondered if we were already on to them. He said he saw them come down here, but I was on the other side waiting for you. They never came out the other end."

"I've been waiting for this for too long now," Bethan heard another voice, low and angry. "I've been letting her walk around here for months like nothing her brother did matters. But playtime's over now. She's got to go down the way our boy did, and then that scumbag will know what it's like and worse. I'm gonna cut her to ribbons."

"Right." The girls heard a third voice.

"Let's find her then," Carter said. "And her little friend. Two for one, bargain."

Kelly and Bethan stared at each other across the expanse of the doorway. The toughened glass didn't seem tough enough any more.

"What about in here?" the second voice said, rattling the door so it shook. "They came in one end and didn't go out the other, which means they must have gone into the tower."

"Press all the doorbells," Carter ordered. "No one's going to hide her from me, not if they've got any sense."

"Someone will let him in any second," Kelly whispered,

gazing wildly around the small foyer, looking for an escape route that didn't exist.

Suddenly there was a ping and the lift doors slid open.

"In there," Kelly whispered.

"And then where?" Bethan asked, just as the buzz of someone releasing the outer lock sounded.

"Quick!"

The girls darted across the lobby and bundled into the lift, pressing the close-door button frantically as Carter and his friends entered.

"In there!" Carter shouted, just as the lift doors slid shut. It lurched upwards, even though neither girl had pressed a button.

"Get it back," they heard him yell, his fist hammering on the metal door. Bethan pressed the button for the highest floor.

"This isn't a way out, it's a trap!" she cried. "He'll stop the lift sooner or later, and he'll be waiting for us. Kelly, what's he going to do when he gets us?"

"I don't know," Kelly said, her eyes filling with tears. "But it's not going to be good. Look, I'll tell him to leave you alone."

"He won't care," Bethan sobbed. "Kelly, think of *something*."

"He'll leave someone down there, waiting for us," Kelly said. "So we can't just go down. He'll be running up the stairs calling the lift. There's nothing we can do but wait. And when the doors open he'll be there. I'm sorry, Bethan."

The girls hugged each other, their eyes tightly shut as they felt the lift shudder to a halt.

"Oh God!" Bethan whispered. The girls clung on to each other, waiting for the doors to open. But they didn't.

"Hang on," Kelly said, looking up. "It's stuck. The lift's stopped between two floors. The doors won't open here."

"Then they can't get in," Bethan breathed. "But how long for?"

Kelly paused; this wasn't like the other night when she had been with Jay and Emily. That had been a power cut. The light had gone off and nothing had worked. Now the lights were on, all the numbers on the display were illuminated, but the lift just wasn't moving. They could hear the sound of Carter and his mates from the floor above.

"Where's it gone? What's happened?" Carter demanded.

"It must be stuck or something," the third voice replied.

"Stuck like sardines in a tin, perfect," Carter said. "Here, see if you can help me get this door open. If they aren't coming out, we'll go in. Oi, girls, we're coming to get you!"

The girls listened to the banging and scuffling above them.

"What's he doing?" Bethan asked.

"He going to try and open the door up there, jump down

153

on to the lift and then get through that." Kelly nodded at the access hatch in the ceiling.

"We need to do something quick. Call the police!" Bethan begged. "They might get here before they get the doors open."

"No, they won't," Kelly said. "Oakhill Estate is the last place they come in a hurry."

"So we're just going to sit and wait for that monster to come in here and… kill us?" Bethan took her mobile out of her pocket.

"Hang on." Kelly picked up the emergency phone. "It probably doesn't work, but perhaps…"

"Hello?" a voice said in her ear. Kelly grinned at Bethan.

"Hello? Me and my friend are stuck in the lift. I don't know which tower we're in, but we're only fifteen and we're really scared. Our parents will be dead worried. Can you send someone really quickly?"

"You're in Oak Tower," the disembodied voice said. "Yeah, I know about you. The engineer should be there any minute."

"Really?" Kelly said, sinking down on her heels, too afraid to feel relieved yet.

"Yep, he radioed in just a moment ago, saying he was on his way. Don't worry, love, we got your call the first time. I'm sorry you've been in there so long, but you're nearly out now, OK?"

"OK," Kelly breathed, putting the phone back, tears rolling down her face as she looked at Bethan, not quite able to trust or believe what she'd just heard. "There's someone coming... I think... I think its going to be OK."

They both jumped as they heard heavy footsteps on the lift roof and the thundering of fists pounding against metal.

"Carter's coming to get you!" they heard a sickening sing-song cry.

"Oi!" They heard a shout from above. "What do you louts think you're doing? That's council property. Get out of there before I report you for vandalism."

"Just try it, Grandad," they heard Carter reply, menace in his voice.

"My dispatch knows exactly where I am," the engineer said. "And see that CCTV up there? It feeds live right back to the security head office, and yes, it is working. I fixed it myself last night. So you try anything, sunshine, and you'll be inside before your feet can touch the ground."

Bethan and Kelly held on to each other tightly as they heard the scrabble of feet.

"Don't worry, girls, we'll be back!" Carter shouted down the shaft.

Bethan gasped as the hatch in the roof opened a few seconds later and the welcome face of the service engineer peered through.

"Hello, ladies. Hope you're not desperate for the loo.

I'm sorry you've been in there so long, but I couldn't get here any sooner. Look, you're only half a metre below floor level. Probably best if I help you out now, otherwise you'll be stuck in there for who knows how long while I get this thing going."

"Is there… is there anyone else out there?" Kelly asked anxiously.

"What, those lads who'd prised the doors open? Trying to impress you, were they? I should stay away from them if I were you; they look like trouble. Don't worry, I sent them packing."

Bethan's legs trembled as she got to her feet. It was only when she saw the tears that were still tracking down Kelly's face, cutting through yesterday's make-up, that she realised how close they had come to… She couldn't bear to think about what could have happened.

"Strange." The engineer scratched his head, quietly pleased that the two girls had decided to stay and watch him work, although he was surprised that they hadn't been keen to get off home as quickly as possible. Still, he never got nearly enough appreciation for what he did and it made a change for the kids round here to actually be interested in something being fixed instead of trying to rip it apart.

"What's strange?" Bethan asked him.

"Well, apart from the damage to the doors those idiots

did, there's nothing wrong with this lift. Nothing at all. As soon as you two got out, it returned itself to the ground floor position and now it's working fine. And what I don't get is you girls say that you were stuck in there for what – about five minutes?"

"Yeah, the longest five minutes of my entire life," Kelly said.

"And it seemed way longer," added Bethan.

"Well – that's what's strange. Control got a call from that lift over an hour ago, from a woman telling him two girls were stuck in a lift and needed help," the engineer told them.

The girls looked at each other. "Maybe someone else was stuck and then the lift starting working again until we got in it and then it broke. Again," Bethan offered.

"Well, I know one thing." The engineer shook his head. "I'm going to be here all day trying to figure it out."

Once they got back to the foyer, Kelly pressed her palms against the glass door. The space seemed empty now. Whatever had been there before, for whatever reason, had gone.

"Carter's still out there looking for me," she said, her gaze sweeping the corridor. "And he's going to be more angry than ever now. Foiled by a baldy, middle-aged lift engineer – that's not exactly the kind of image he's going for."

"And we're still on the wrong side of the estate,"

Bethan pointed out anxiously. Never had her life swung between two such extremes before, one minute caught up in something that seemed paranormal, the next faced with the all too real world of dirt and death and violence that she knew was always going on somewhere round here. For once in her life, Bethan felt grateful to her parents for everything they did to try and shield her, and she pitied Kelly and Emily for not having the same kind of protection, unless…

"You could call your dad?" Bethan suggested.

"Are you joking?" Kelly said bitterly. "He'll have been in the pub since opening."

Bethan thought for a moment. "Right, well, we'll call my dad. He'll come and get us."

"I don't know," Bethan's dad said jovially as he manoeuvred the car out of the walkway and back on to the road that circled the estate. "You walk all the way to here and *then* decide you need a lift? Why didn't you call me this morning like I told you to?"

"I wish I had," Bethan said, more to herself than to her father. Then she had a thought. "Dad – Kelly's coming back for lunch and then we're going to watch DVDs and she'll probably stay over. You don't mind, do you? You and Mum are going out and it'll be nice for me to have a friend over, won't it?"

"Yes, love, that's great." Bethan's dad sounded surprised and pleased all at once that Bethan finally seemed to have found a friend she wanted to bring home.

Bethan glanced at Kelly to see what she thought of the invitation, but Kelly was staring out of the window. After a second though, Bethan felt Kelly's fingers reach for hers and without looking, she took Bethan's and squeezed them.

Bethan squeezed back.

CHAP✝ER ELEVEN

As he waited in the old history block, Jay watched the footage from the camcorder on his laptop for about the hundredth time since he'd first transferred it on Saturday afternoon. All weekend he'd studied and studied it, resisting the urge to call the others in until he'd tried every possible way to explain what was on there. He still couldn't believe what he was seeing, and if he couldn't even believe *his* eyes then what were the others going to think?

He'd gone over and over the piece of footage, looking for anomalies, wondering how what he was seeing could have possibly happened. A power surge maybe, or a light flare? But that wouldn't produce an image as clear as this one. And this was digital camera, so there was no film to be corrupted or negative to be altered. This wasn't just a so-called orb, and he couldn't get the image out of his mind. Even when the laptop was turned off, closed tightly and shut away in his wardrobe with a chair pulled in front of it. Jay couldn't quite shake the feeling that what was captured inside might at any moment climb out of the monitor and into the room, to come and get him.

An orb was usually a small ball of light that some paranormal investigators claimed was the first sign of the manifestation of a ghost. More often than not, from what Jay had seen online, the image could just as easily be a moth drawn to a bulb, or a piece of floating dust reflecting the camera's light. But what Jay could not stop picturing, even when he shut his eyes and tried to sleep, was no moth. No, this was much more. And that was truly terrifying.

Jay made himself look at the image again. Staring back at him, with burning eyes that seemed to see him from the other side of the screen, and possibly even the other side of death, was a woman's face. A face wrought and distorted with anguish and anger. A face he didn't know, who certainly hadn't been in Emily's house on Friday night and who, if he was right, was a ghost caught on camera in the most shocking and vivid detail.

Closing the laptop again, Jay thought of all the images of so-called ghosts he'd looked up on the internet while he was getting ready to investigate Emily's house. There had been hours of footage of orbs and some films of furniture appearing to move. A few posts here and there showed a shadowy figure passing through a wall, and there were loads that were clearly rigged up as a joke to spook anyone who watched them. All of the clips could be explained away as being caused by something other than a ghost, most often by the computer expertise of whoever posted the clips. But not this. Jay was fairly certain that this had only one explanation, one that he couldn't deny any longer.

He was looking at a real ghost; a ghost that could well be Emily's mum.

The question was, how did he tell the others what he had found? And worst of all, how did he show Emily the very thing that might prove her mother was dead?

"All right?" Hashim was the first to turn up. "Bring my camcorder back? Mum gave me non-stop hassle about lending it to you all weekend."

Jay nodded and pushed the camera across the desk towards Hashim.

"So, anything good on it?" Hashim asked as he picked the device up and zipped it in his bag. "Did we catch Emily creeping into her mum's room when none of us was looking?"

Jay shook his head and swallowed. "We'd better wait for the others to arrive before I tell you," he said.

"Tell me what? Jay, man, you OK? You look like you've seen a…" Hashim shut his mouth and looked around the room as if he expected someone else to be there. "You look well freaked."

"I am fully freaked," Jay assured him.

Before he could say any more, Bethan and Kelly arrived. They had arrived at school together too, Jay had noticed. They had trooped in through the gate as if suddenly they were best friends. Kelly hadn't hung with her usual gang at break and something seemed different about her. About them both. They looked jumpy and nervous, standing on their own in the corner of the playground, talking in low voices, constantly glancing over their shoulders. If Jay hadn't known better he would have said they had already seen the camcorder footage.

"Hey," said Jay, smiling tentatively at Kelly, and was touched and surprised by her answering smile which was just as cautious.

"Hi," the two girls said together, sitting side by side.

"So what's the deal?" Hashim grinned, looking them up and down. "Has Hell frozen over or something? Are there pigs flying around in the sky?"

"What are you on about?" Bethan asked him.

"You two, all kissy best mates and that. Don't get me wrong, I'm all for the impossible becoming possible, it's just – you two? Really?"

"Don't be a plank," Kelly said, but without her usual venom. "It's no big deal. Beth's all right, that's all."

"Right," Hashim said, taken aback by Kelly's mild response. He didn't know quite how to deal with her when she didn't have her claws out. "Cool."

"Is Emily coming?" Jay asked them uncomfortably.

"Haven't seen her all day," said Bethan.

"Right," Jay looked thoughtfully at his PC.

"Right what?" Bethan asked impatiently. "Have you got something? What did the camcorder show?"

Jay opened the machine, turned it to face the others and pressed play.

For a while after it had finished, the four sat in silence, unable to look at each other.

"Look, I know what you're thinking," Jay said into the silence. "But I swear to you I didn't touch that recording. I did nothing to it. All I did was feed it from the camcorder to the laptop, and that is what was there. It's still on the camcorder too."

"Is it?" Hashim asked. He glanced uncomfortably at his bag.

"And I know you're going to think I'm crazy, but I thought and thought about it and I think that *is* a ghost. That Emily isn't mad and there is a ghost in her house. And, well, what if it's Emily's mum trying to reach her? God knows that's the last thing I expected to think. I'd have said it was a parallel universe crossing over with ours before I said that ghosts were real, but now… I can't find any other explanation. So go on, call me a nutter." Jay lifted his chin, bracing himself for the ridicule.

"I believe you," Hashim said. "What I don't get is why I didn't see her."

"I knew you— *What?*" Jay was thrown by Hashim's answer.

"And I believe you too," Kelly said, looking at Bethan, who nodded.

"Me too."

"But why?" Jay was incredulous. He was so sure that the others would accuse him of rigging the tape for effect, or call him a freak and a geek, like they did whenever he talked about any of his pet subjects. But they were sitting there as serious and as scared as he had ever seen them. And they believed him.

"We think – strike that – we *know* that a ghost, maybe that ghost, followed us back from Emily's on Saturday…" Bethan nodded at the screen. "We heard and saw things that… well, they weren't normal, put it that way. Somehow the ghost, whatever it was, knew something we didn't and tried to warn us. Why would it do that? Unless it is Emily's mum, unless it knows we are trying to help her and it decided to help us."

"Either that or this town's full of ghosts," said Kelly.

"What happened to you exactly?" Jay asked, desperate for another piece of the puzzle that seemed to make less sense the more of the picture he could see.

Kelly and Bethan described what had happened to them

after they had left Emily's house, constantly glancing at each other for reassurance.

"And the lift engineer was called an hour before you were trapped?" Jay asked. "How is that possible?"

"Well, maybe ghosts can time-travel," Bethan suggested.

"That's incredible," Jay breathed.

"Yeah, but I didn't see her. I didn't seeing anything the whole night." Hashim looked confused, but not as confused as the others.

"What *are* you going on about?" Kelly asked him with a reassuring touch of her old impatience.

Hashim paused. "Well, I thought I had a brain tumour. Sort of *hoped* I had one really. But I know it's not that. I see people that no one else can see. I see… ghosts. Like, all the time."

The others stared at him open-mouthed, but none of them laughed or scoffed.

"How?" Jay asked. "Why? *When?*"

"Well, remember that night we broke into the science lab?" Hashim told Jay about the figure of the man that he'd seen loitering in the corner when the lights had gone out.

"*That's* why you wanted to get out of there so quickly," Jay said. "I've never seen you scared before."

"I'm not usually scared," Hashim said, with some bravado. "It's not even the first time I've seen him. That

166

time he was actually quite cool, gave me some footy tips. But this time there was something else. He was…" Hashim struggled to find the right word. "Menacing. Threatening, y'know?"

"But you didn't see a ghost at Emily's house," stated Bethan.

"No, and I don't see them all the time. There's not one here now, for example."

"Good, cos I'm well over ghosts," Kelly muttered.

"And when you two went off together on Saturday morning, I didn't see one following you. But that man, the bloke in the school, is different from the others I've seen. He's the only one who's ever looked at me, or talked to me. The others – it's kind of like they're photographs. Like memories. They don't see me – they don't see the world around them at all. They don't know they're dead."

"When did this start?" Bethan asked him, confused. "Did you have a near-death experience or something? Is there a long line of ghost spotters in your family?"

"It started a few months back, and no, I haven't nearly died, unless you count the time I dislocated my knee in a sliding tackle – *that* felt like I was dying. I have no idea why me or why now. It's totally random as far as I can see, but it is real."

"You know what the really freaky thing is," Kelly said. "We totally believe you, you bizarre, corpse-seeing freak."

"Thanks for that, Kel," said Hashim. "Great to have your support." But the truth was it was great to have told them. It was a massive relief, just like when the physio popped his knee back in after that tackle. Yeah, things were getting weirder and scarier by the second, but now he had people to talk to. People who believed him. It felt good.

"There are supposed to be different types of ghosts," Jay nodded, like Kelly needing no further explanation or proof from Hashim. "Some, like you said, are supposed to be like imprints on time. Bits of video on a constant loop, playing over and over again. I read about this housemaid that constantly walks up and down the stairs in the old house she used to work in. They're the stairs she fell down and broke her neck on. And in Scotland there's this old road where quite often the locals say they hear and see regiments of Roman centurions marching to their doom. Except they're only seen from the waist up because the level of the road has risen since Roman times, but the ghosts don't know that; they just keep marching."

"Yeah, but people die all the time. Why aren't they all walking around?" Kelly asked. "Why aren't we always seeing or hearing things?"

"I'm not so sure that we're not," said Bethan. "I wonder if we've just got so used to it, that we ignore it most of the time, because it's easier than dealing with it. I'm not the only one who sees things out of the corner of my eye, am I?

You all do, don't you? It's this place. It's Woodsville. *Weird*sville."

The others didn't speak, but they didn't deny it either.

"There are lots of theories about why a haunting happens." Jay spoke into the silence. "When a death is violent or unexpected, some people believe that it's the emotion and shock that causes imprints on the place. And some say that the most haunted places are situated on ley lines, which are supposedly like invisible psychic power connections that run up and down the whole country. A lot of people reckon they act like generators, giving ghosts the energy to manifest. Often haunted places are found to have really high electromagnetic fields, a sort of radiation that comes from the earth and the rocks, which is why we took the EMF readers in the first place. Studies have shown that high levels of electromagnetic energy can cause a person to feel frightened and to hallucinate. Some footage has even shown it to be strong enough to move objects slightly. But the question is, does it simply heighten the senses of the living to the world of the dead? Are the walls between time and space a little thinner in places like that?"

Jay paused for breath, aware that he was going on a bit.

"Well, explain then, brainiac," Kelly demanded. Jay felt flattered; he wasn't sure Kelly had ever been interested in anything he'd ever had to say before. He liked it.

"Yeah, what about the other types of ghosts. Ghosts like

Hashim's creepy bloke and her, that woman, whoever she is." Bethan nodded at the laptop.

"They're called active ghosts or earthbound spirits," Jay explained. "Ghosts who are trapped on earth, who know they are dead, but either can't or don't want to 'cross over' to wherever it is they go. They try and interact with humans. Some are trying to get attention by scaring people; others are trying to resolve something so that they can leave. If our ghost was that type of ghost – and I'm fairly sure she is – then Hashim probably didn't see her because active ghosts can control their manifestation. They're only seen if they want to be."

"And that would be her," Hashim said. "Cos I'd say transporting your daughter through a wall was pretty active."

"Hang on, we don't *know* that she's Emily's mother," Jay said. "That house is old. I bet a load of people have died there. It could just be that the ghost picked on Emily because it knows her, or because she's alone and vulnerable."

"I think we do know," Kelly said quietly. "We do know that it's Emily's mother."

"What do you mean?" Jay asked her.

Calmly, Kelly opened Jay's laptop again. She rewound the film a few frames so that an image of the windowsill was visible. Then, after a bit of fiddling around, she zoomed in on something standing there.

"Can you make this focus?" she asked Jay.

"Yes, a little bit," Jay said. "Press 'image enhance'."

"There." Kelly stepped back and the others crowded round. They were looking at the photo that stood in a frame on the windowsill. It wasn't perfectly sharp, but it was clearly a photo of Emily and a woman, smiling at the camera, their arms wrapped around each other. The same woman who only seconds later was staring into the camera lens.

"Whoa!" Hashim gasped.

"So what do we do now?" Bethan asked. "Go round Emily's and tell her that her mum is dead and haunting her. And, by the way, she's really ticked off?"

"No! God, no," Kelly said. "The last thing we do is tell Emily. If your mum was missing, would that be the way you'd want to find out that she was dead? We need to fix this first. We need to find out how to help the ghost, and how to help Emily deal with this nightmare."

The others looked at her in surprise; none of them recognised this sensitive side of Kelly – but all of them liked it.

"But we know that her mum must be dead. We can't hide *that* from her!" Bethan argued. "We should tell people – the school, social services… the police."

"And show them our video of a dead woman?" Kelly scoffed. "Look, we all know what's going on and we all get it, but they'd laugh in our faces. We need help, but not that kind of help."

"I know someone who can help us," Jay said, chewing his lip.

"Who?" asked Hashim.

"My grandad," Jay told them.

"Your grandad? I haven't seen him around the estate since I was a kid. I thought he was dead," Bethan said.

"He is, mostly," Jay told her.

CHAP✝ER ✝WELVE

Albert Romero wasn't actually dead of course. It was more that he'd given up on living. Jay's mum said it wasn't surprising that his grandad had decided to become a virtual hermit, what with everything that had happened to him. About five years ago, after a lifetime of smoking had blocked the main arteries to his legs, Albert had to have both of them amputated because they were slowly dying and threatened to take him with them as they decayed. And not long after that, Albert and Jay's dad had fallen out and hadn't talked since. Jay wasn't sure what the argument was about and nobody at home would tell him. In fact, the one time he had questioned his dad about it had also been the one time his dad had ever walloped him, so he hadn't brought it up again.

Albert, who lived on the top floor of Cherry Tree Tower, had also given up on most people. He couldn't get on with the artificial limbs he'd been given. He told Jay that his "phantom legs" still pained him, even though they were long gone, incinerated in the hospital furnace the same afternoon as the surgeon had lopped them off. After Albert and Jay's dad fell out so violently, neither Jay nor his mother had ever been able to persuade the two to talk again and Albert simply gave up going out. And, as Jay's mum said, nobody could blame him. It wasn't as if there were anything worth that much effort to see in Woodsville, even with two good legs.

Jay's mum did his shopping, dropping in food once a week, and two carers from an old people's charity called in twice a day to help him wash and keep the place clean. Not that Albert was grateful. He had the highest turnover of carers out of all of the charity's old people. Most of them couldn't stand his morbid talk and some of them just found him plain scary.

Jay wasn't surprised that Bethan had thought his grandfather was dead. He hadn't been seen out on the estate for years, and the many friends that he used to have had dropped away one by one. But Jay was always a regular visitor to his grandad. Yes, with his rotten, gap-toothed grin and the eyepatch he'd worn since his twenties, having lost his eye under circumstances that were never quite clear, Albert did look like a demented pirate. An effect that wasn't helped by his long hair, which was silver at the roots and yellow at the tips, where the nicotine from his endless chain-smoking had stained it. He also smelt a bit funny, of stale smoke and stout ale, but Albert knew things. He knew things about subjects that nobody would ever expect, to look at him.

Albert knew all sorts of facts on science, space travel, plant life, the history of the town, the history of the world. He seemed to have read every book that had ever been written; he could tell you all about every war that had ever been fought from the Greeks to Iraq.

When Jay was a very little boy, he'd taken everything his grandad had told him as fact. But after his dad had made some snide comment about Albert knowing every-thing – if everything counted as whatever he made up off the top of his head – Jay had started randomly checking his grandad's information. And so far, he had never found Albert to be wrong. Which led him to conclude that his mad, demented piratey, smelly old grandad was some-thing of a genius, and the only person Jay had ever met who had the same lust for knowledge that he had. Not that it stopped Albert from being a miserable old sod though.

Whenever Jay visited, Albert would more often than not stare bleakly into his tea and tell Jay that he was waiting to die. Actually, the last time Jay had been there, about a week earlier, he'd said a bit more than that. He'd said,

"Well, at least I'll be one of them soon and then maybe they'll leave me alone."

"What are you on about, Gramps?" Jay asked. He'd brought his grandad's favourite humbug mints, the ones that had probably contributed to the loss of his teeth over the years.

Albert's appearance and his often gloomy and dark comments made it no surprise that local kids frequently made special trips to the top floor of Cherry Tree Tower to torment him. Ringing his bell, knocking on his door and calling him a witch, a zombie and a kid-killer through the letter box. Confronting the mad old bloke in Flat 229 had become something of a rite of passage for the pre-teen kids of the block, and they would add to Albert's undeserved bogeyman status by telling each other terrifying stories. Like how he prowled the corridors of his floor by night in his wheelchair, and how he kept the kids he caught in a chest freezer in his bedroom before he ate them.

None of this was true of course. Albert was grumpy, but he wasn't psychotic. He was just like anyone else's grandad, if anyone else's grandad hated people and said a lot of strange things. But Jay didn't think it was such a bad thing that most of the local kids grew up being frightened of Albert, because a lot of them grew up to be criminals too, and so far Albert's was one of the few flats in the block that hadn't been turned over at least once.

"I mean the ghosts, and worse, that are everywhere, waiting. When I'm dead, I'm going over. Whatever they try. I'm going over if it kills me, and I'm staying there. Where they can't get at me."

"The kids, you mean?" Jay asked.

"The dead ones anyway," Albert had replied, popping a mint into his mouth and sinking into silence as he sucked it into nothingness.

"I did my bit," Albert had said after several moments of sucking. "I fought them most of my life. I told your father that it was his turn now. That he had to be a man and take on his destiny, but he wouldn't. He never believed. Never wanted to believe, not even what he saw with his own eyes. But then that's what it's like these days; everyone's switched off their brains. They don't want to believe that there's more to this world than work and bills and fish and chips on a Friday night. Most of them don't know what living is. They're sleepwalking. But if they don't wake up soon, they'll be dead a lot quicker than they realise and it won't be no picnic then. It won't be bright lights and tunnels and fluffy clouds. It'll be dark and cold and a never-ending hell. But no one listens, no one, so why should I? I won't be here. I'll be long gone before it all kicks off."

"Grandad," Jay had said carefully, "you say a lot of this 'the end is nigh' and the 'world is doomed' sort of stuff, but you never really explain what you mean. You say that no one listens, but I do. Only I have no idea what you're going on about. If you could just, you know, *tell* me, maybe I could help."

Albert had looked at Jay for a long time with his one good eye.

"I would tell you, but you're not ready yet," he said. "Don't you know I'm only hanging on for you now? If I haven't kicked the bucket by the time you're ready, then maybe, just maybe, if you're strong enough, you'll be able to hold back the dark for a little while longer. Do the job that the Romeros have been doing for centuries. Until your father, that is, the good-for-nothing waste of space…"

Jay had listened to Albert's rant about his dad for a few more minutes and then walked home, wondering how the man that his grandad despised so much could be his dad. His mild-mannered, bad-joke-telling father, who worked at the car plant like everyone else and never had a bad word to say about anyone. Except Albert.

Most of the people that spent any time with Albert thought he was just a bit loopy. A bitter old man whose mind was descending into death quicker than the rest of him, just like his legs had. But that wasn't how Jay felt. He had always known in his gut that there was something more in Woodsville, something constantly in the shadows. Like most people, he hadn't wanted to see it, but he had always wondered. Now he *knew*. He knew that ghosts were real. Maybe he was right about parallel universes, maybe he wasn't. But what he was certain of was that ghosts existed in this universe. They hung around, sometimes without even knowing it, and they were everywhere. So if there was anyone who would know what to do, it would be Albert. Which made him exactly the kind of help they needed.

"I don't like this," Kelly sniffed as they stepped out of the lift and on to his grandad's floor.

"What's the difference between this and any other floor in any other tower block?" Bethan asked.

"None, I s'pose," Kelly said, but nevertheless she eyed the flickering light above Albert's front door with caution. "It just feels like we're not alone."

Hashim paused, staring down the corridor into the shadows at the bottom where the lights had given up completely.

"We're not," he said. "There's a woman down there who's trying to get into her flat, only she can't make the key work."

"What wom— oh." Jay shut his mouth as he realised Hashim was seeing one of his dead people. "And she can't see us?"

"If she can, she doesn't care," Hashim said, swallowing

as he kept his eyes on what the rest of them couldn't see. "She looks scared. Looks like she wants to get indoors before something really bad happens. I wonder how long she's been trying."

"I'd like to get in somewhere now, if you don't mind," Kelly said in a small voice that was so unlike her it made everyone's head swivel in her direction.

"What? I've just had enough of ghosts for five minutes. I am, like, fully over dead people. Are you telling me you aren't?"

No one protested, so Jay knocked three times on the door like he always did and then used his key to let himself in.

"Gramps?" he called out as he walked into the narrow hallway. "I've brought some friends to meet you."

Albert was sitting with his back to them as they walked into his living room, his head lolling sideways at an awkward angle.

"Gramps?" Jay said loudly, but the old man didn't move.

"Oh my God, he's not…?" Kelly whispered.

"Grandad?" Jay's voice wobbled as he edged closer to Albert's motionless body. Gingerly he reached out and grabbed one of the chair handles. Taking a deep breath, he spun the chair round to face him. One bloodshot eye stared at him, unblinking.

"Hell, he's—"

"BOO!" Albert shouted before nearly choking on his own laughter.

"Grandad!" Jay yelled. "You do my head in!"

"Every time!" Albert's chuckle rattled wheezily in his chest. "He falls for it every time! Oh, don't be so soft, lad. I'm just having a bit of a joke with you. Don't worry about it. When I'm really dead, you'll be the first to know. I'll tell you myself. Now, who's this lot? You know I don't like visitors."

"Are you crazy?" Kelly asked, clutching her chest. "We thought you'd copped it!"

"I bet he didn't." Albert nodded at Hashim. He scrutinised Jay with his one good eye. "Why have you brought these yobs to see me, Jay? What's happened?"

"They aren't yobs," Jay said defensively. "They're my friends."

He hesitated, but no one, not even Kelly, contradicted him so he felt safe to continue. "And we've got involved in something… weird. You're the only person I could think of who might know what to do next."

"Well, spit it out then," Albert said. "I haven't got all day. I might not have the next five minutes, the state my ticker's in."

Jay put his laptop on the table and began.

Albert was so still when Jay stopped talking that Jay wondered if he really was dead this time. "So what do you think?" Jay nodded at the laptop. "Do you think that's real?"

"That's real all right," Albert said. "Funny, I always thought all this techno-hokum was a waste of time. Didn't know you could *video* the beggars. That would have made life a lot easier in my day. Then again, that's the trouble with you lot. Don't know you're born."

"You don't seem very shocked by the fact we've videoed a ghost," Bethan quizzed, sitting down across the table from Albert as if she was nervous that he might jump out of his chair and chase after her on his stumps.

"Shocked? I'm pleased, love."

"You're pleased?" scowled Kelly. "Pleased that Emily's mum is dead and haunting her? *Sick.*"

"It's very sad, but people die. Did you know that in Woodsville the rate of accidental death is seven per cent higher than the national average? The murder rate is sixteen per cent higher and we get more cancer round here too. They used to try and blame it on the water, the power plant, even the mobile phone masts, but so far they've never proved anything. Except that death feels at home in Woodsville. So I'm sorry and sad for the young lady, but I'm not surprised. Because not only do people die more often than not round here, they can get caught in the... in the *branches* and can't get away as easily as they should be able to." Albert nodded at the laptop. "In this case, this lady either doesn't want to or can't go until she's got a message to your friend... what's her name again?"

"Emily," Jay reminded him. He was watching Albert with interest. It had been a long time since he'd seen his grandad looking so... well, *alive*. His skin was flushed, he was sitting up in his chair and his eye was even sparkling.

"Well, Emily's mum might have something really profound to tell her, like where she keeps the money or that her dad is the prime minister, or it might be something small, like she forgot to pay the gas bill or hoover under the bed. It doesn't really matter what the message is. When you're dead, telling your loved ones what you didn't get a chance to when you were alive becomes your reason for staying around." Albert glanced at the still face that had been caught so vividly on the camcorder. "In this case, I think it's easy enough to guess what she wants to say. She just wants to tell her little girl what's happened."

Albert glanced up at Hashim. "What's your name, son?" he asked, his tone uncharacteristically gentle.

"Hashim, sir."

"Hashim. If my memory serves me right that means Destroyer of Evil," Albert nodded. "Good name."

"Thank you, sir."

"You can see them, can't you. Ghosts."

Hashim nodded. "How can you tell?"

"I recognise the look. Jumpy – haunted. Used to work with a feller like you. I know how hard it can be, some of the things you see."

"I didn't always see them," Hashim said, looking at Albert. "It started a few months back."

"Something happened then. Something or someone kick-started your psychic ability. Question is how, and why now? We'll need to find that out at some point. But don't feel too much of an oddball, son. All of us could see them if we tried. Every now and then we see them when we don't try, if they're powerful enough. But who wants to try and see the things you do, right?"

"I know I could live without it," Hashim sighed.

"You say you didn't see Emily's mum until she was on the tape."

Hashim nodded.

"And you girls think it was her that followed you, helped you escape from this Carter, but you didn't see anything at all?"

"No," Kelly said.

Bethan nodded. "We heard breathing though and footsteps and a voice that could have been a woman's voice telling us to hide. And if that wasn't Emily's mum, then who was it? Who else—"

"Interesting," Albert said, cutting her off.

"So?" Jay asked him. "What do we do now, Grandad?"

Albert looked thoughtful for a moment. "Often when something really bad happens, the human brain just chooses not to remember it. It decides to shut that part of itself down and forget about it. It's possible that Emily knows more about what happened to her mother than she can remember. You say she's lived on her own for weeks now without telling a living soul? And she's kept it quiet because she doesn't want to go back into care, but you'd think she'd want to find her mother, whatever the cost. Unless she knows what's happened, but she can't remember."

"You mean she's lying?" Bethan asked him.

"No, not lying. She just can't remember the truth because it's…"

"Too awful to remember?" Kelly finished for him.

Kelly had been far too young to remember the day that her mother had vanished, but when she was little she used to tell herself that on that day her mum had taken her out to the park and walked her to the pond to feed the ducks. Kelly had always imagined herself wearing a pink dress and a matching sun hat, that the sky was blue and she felt the warmth of the sun bathing her skin. Her mother had told her that she loved her, and that Kelly was the most precious thing in her life. She didn't want to go, but she *had* to.

It was only when Kelly was much older that she realised she'd never owned a pink dress or a matching sun hat. Her mother had vanished out of her life on a freezing February morning without saying a word to anyone. Once the dream had been shattered by the truth, Kelly had mourned its loss. She could understand why Emily might not want to remember anything she might know about her mum's disappearance.

"Oh. My. God," Bethan said slowly. "I've worked it out. Emily murdered her mum!"

"You what?" There was a moment of stunned silence, then they all laughed.

"Emily Night? She couldn't murder a cheese sandwich, let alone an actual person!" exclaimed Hashim.

"Couldn't she? I mean, isn't she exactly the sort of person who would? A loner, always polite, but never socialises. Weird-looking."

"Mate," Kelly said, "you've just described yourself."

"And me, for that matter," Jay added. "Emily loved her mum. She was the only person she had in the world. Whatever it is she's afraid to remember, I don't think it's murder."

"So how do you ask a person what it is they don't remember?" Bethan looked at Albert.

"By not asking them. You've got to try and find out a bit more about Emily. Have a look round her place, see if there's anything there that might tell you what's happened."

"So we ask her to let us in so we can search the place?" Hashim's laugh was mirthless.

"I didn't say *ask*!" Albert scrutinised the four of them.

"Grandad, are you telling us we should break into her house?" asked Jay in horror. "That's illegal!"

"Good God, boy, you're more like your father than I thought. In this job sometimes you have to bend the rules a bit. And sometimes you have to smash them into pieces. It's not as if you're doing it to hurt or steal from Emily, is it? You're doing it to help her."

"In what way?" Jay was confused.

"That house would be easy to break into," Kelly mused. "Only one lock on the front door. You just need a credit card for that type…" The others stared at her.

"You don't grow up with a brother like mine without picking up on some stuff," she shrugged. "All we'd have to do is to make sure that Emily is out."

"Easy, I'll invite her round to mine for a girly night," Bethan said. "While she's with me, I'll try and find out a bit more about her, while you lot look round her place."

"Are you *sure* this is the best thing to do, Grandad?" Jay looked uncertainly at Albert.

"When if comes to stuff like this, son, there's no easy way to sort it. You can't get a book out of the library or look it up on that interweb. You have to find out what happened to Emily's mum and help her find peace before… before it's too late for her to go anywhere and she ends up trapped here. Like I told your dad, it's a dirty job, but…" Albert trailed off. "You've got to do what you've got to do."

"I'm up for it," said Hashim. "Emily's house is one of the few places I've been recently where I *haven't* seen one of them."

"Me too," Kelly said. "I'm not scared of nothing."

"I can see that," Albert said approvingly. "You're the warrior."

"And you'll be OK on your own with Emily? You know, considering she's an axe murderer," Jay teased Bethan.

"Actually, women are far more likely to poison than chop," Bethan said primly. Adding, "You're not the only one who knows stuff."

"Well, we've got to do *something*," Jay said, feeling an uncomfortable churning in the pit of his stomach. "So it might as well be this."

CHAP✟ER ✟HIR✟EEN

*T*he trouble with Emily was that she was hard to get hold of. After they had left Albert's flat, the four of them had gone back to Jay's to talk over their plans.

"Hello, son," his mother had said, raising her eyebrows as Jay tramped into the flat with a group of friends for the first time since he was about ten, and two girls in tow for the first time ever.

"Hi, Mum. We're just gonna go in my room and... um, do some homework. It's like a group project thing," Jay told her. "OK?"

"Yes, love, of course." Jay's mum followed them down the corridor, scarcely able to conceal her pleasure in her son's unexpected social life. "Can I bring you anything? Some juice maybe, or I've got some custard creams in the larder..."

"No thanks, we're going to be very busy," Jay said,

holding his bedroom door open as the others tramped in.

Only Hashim paused. "Thanks for having us, Mrs Romero," he said, smiling sweetly.

"It's my pleasure, love. Now what about some—" But the sentence was never finished as Jay shut the door firmly.

"I'll call Emily and ask her over for tea tonight," Bethan said, fishing her phone out of her school bag. "Then you lot can go and turn over her house."

"Investigate it for clues," Jay corrected her.

"What the hell is *that*?" Kelly asked, nodding at a model spaceship that hung from Jay's ceiling on a thin piece of cotton.

"That… it's… er, a model of the Millennium Falcon from *Star Wars*." Jay's response was a mixture of pride and embarrassment. "I made it a couple of years ago. Took me *weeks*. And those…" He nodded at a collection of model aeroplanes that were hung from the ceiling as if engaged in a dogfight. "Messerschmitts and spitfires, exact replicas of the ones that were in the Battle of Britain, summer 1940. On that day…"

"Yeah, all right, geek out," Kelly said. "God, you are into fully lame stuff."

"At least I'm *into* stuff," Jay snapped back unexpectedly. "At least I don't spend my whole life yacking on about telly and boys and who said what to who and why."

"I'd be worried if you did spend the whole day going on about boys," Hashim joked, eliciting a smirk from Kelly that made Jay feel even more irritable.

"There nothing wrong with being gay," Bethan chided, still clutching her phone.

"I'm *not* gay though!" exclaimed Jay.

"Yes, but if you were there's nothing wrong with it. I'd still be your friend." Bethan smiled at him sweetly.

"And me. Gay guys are cool," Kelly added. "But you're definitely not gay, because gay geeks are genetically impossible, and anyway, they'd never wear *this*." She picked up a bright green jumper that Jay's mum had bought him because she said it matched his eyes.

"Hang on, I am *not* gay and I am *not* a geek," Jay protested. "And since when did this become a pick-on-Jay day? Haven't we got a ghost to find and a girl to help, who doesn't yet know that her mother might be dead?"

Kelly sighed. "Of course we have. I just thought I'd take a five-minute break from being up to my ears in spooky deadness and breaking and entering. I fancied being normal – and picking on you is normal."

"Oh, right." Jay felt oddly quite pleased that Kelly had chosen him to take her mind off things. He'd started this whole ghost-hunt thing as a way to get closer to her, never expecting it to work. But here they were, up to their ears in spooky deadness, as Kelly put it, and they were definitely closer. They shared a bond, a common purpose and a friendship that one day might become something more. "No worries."

"You are a geek though," Kelly added, treating Jay to such a dazzling smile that he thought he might never speak again.

"Come on, it's getting late. I'll have to invite Emily for a midnight feast at this rate," Bethan reminded them. "Who's got Emily's number?"

It was then they realised that no one did. Eventually Jay remembered that his mum kept a phone book in a drawer in the front room. He slid silently along the hallway, making sure that his mum was safely in the kitchen and that his dad was snoring in front of the telly. He didn't need to be secretive about it of course; it was just that if his mum saw him, she'd start asking questions and he'd have to tell her another lie, and Jay hated lying to his mother. Unlike Bethan, he was happy to share everything that happened in his life – this was the first time that he couldn't.

They found Emily's house number in the phone book. Bethan dialled and the others waited. "It's disconnected," she said, looking at her phone. "I guess Emily hasn't paid the bill since her mum's been gone."

"So what do we do now?" Hashim asked. "Go round there?"

"Don't think there's anything else we can do…"

Just then there was a knock at the door.

"Mum, I said we didn't want any—" Jay opened it to find Emily standing there. He let out a yelp of surprise.

"Hi," Emily said, peering into the room. "Oh, you're all here. I thought I'd come round and see if you found anything on the camera."

"Emily, cool!" Bethan said, collecting herself when she realised that no one was going to speak. The others just sat staring, suddenly remembering that this was a real girl they were dealing with. A girl who was going to have to come to terms with the fact that her mother was not only dead, but stuck in the spirit world trying to tell her something. When Emily wasn't there, this whole thing was weird and difficult and scary, but it didn't seem real. Now she'd actually arrived, they were at a loss, knowing what they knew and with no idea how to tell her.

"I was just trying to call you," Bethan babbled on as Emily advanced cautiously into the room, the door swinging shut behind her. "I thought how bored and lonely you must be stuck in that house and I wondered if you fancied coming over to mine tonight. Now, more or less, for tea and some girly DVDs and things…" Bethan trailed off, a fixed grin stretching from ear to ear.

"Really?" Emily asked her. "Tonight?"

"Yes, I was just trying to phone you, but the line's cut off." Bethan looked at her phone. "Damn, it's gone flat. It was fully charged this morning. Now I won't be able to phone mum and tell her I'm bringing a friend back."

"Here, use… Oh, mine's gone too," Kelly said, looking at Hashim, who took his phone out of his back pocket.

"Dead." Hashim looked carefully around the room. There was a moment's silence as everybody had the same thought at the same moment. Emily's mother was here and for some reason didn't want them to use their phones.

"So what about the recording?" Emily asked.

"It's clear, as far as I can see." Hashim shook his head, noticing the sudden chill in the air.

"Clear of what?" Emily paled. "Did you see anything?"

"Not exactly," Jay stepped in. Grandad said they had to get Emily to remember what had happened the day her mum disappeared. If they told her too much too soon, it might mess things up and then they'd never find a way of helping Emily's mum talk to her.

"It wasn't clear, but it did show that you weren't tricking us. It showed that whatever happened, it was definitely paranormal."

"Paranormal." Emily sat down on the edge of Jay's bed and suddenly the room seemed smaller. It felt crowded with misery. Fear, regret and confusion swirled, as palpable as the outward puff of breath that had begun to crystallise in the fast-chilling air. "Does that means that Mum's—?"

"We don't know," Jay said hastily. "We don't know what it means, but we're going to find out. We are trying really hard, Emily. I'm sorry we haven't been in touch today, but when you weren't at school—"

"I just want her back. I just want my mum." Emily's voice trembled and the light bulb above their heads flickered. Jay looked at Hashim, who shrugged. He couldn't see Emily's mum anywhere in the room, but then again, he hadn't seen her at Emily's house either. Whatever kind of ghost she was, it was a kind that he couldn't see.

"I know," Kelly said, sitting next to Emily and shivering as she put an arm around the girl's bony shoulders. She looked at Jay. "All of this is because she wants us to tell her everything," Kelly chose her words carefully. She was sure that if Emily's mother was in the room then she was angry that the people who were supposed to be helping her daughter were keeping her in the dark. The only way Kelly could think of to stop that was to tell Emily the truth, whether she was ready to hear it or not.

Jay shook his head.

"Is that everything?" Emily looked at Bethan, her dark eyes burning, but not with tears.

"Of course. Look, come home with me now," Bethan replied, taking Emily's hand. "We'll watch soppy films and take our minds off it all for a bit." She glanced around the room, adding pointedly, "I'm sure that wherever your mum is, she wouldn't want you to be upset."

And in that second the atmosphere changed, just a fraction. The light bulb steadied to its normal, friendly, yellow beam, the room warmed up and the feelings of fear and anger evaporated.

"You're all being so kind to me." Emily smiled weakly. Kelly buried her head in her hands and Jay and Hashim looked at their feet.

"Not kind, we're just helping. Like we promised," Bethan told her. "Everything we do, we're trying to make this… better."

Kelly waited until Bethan and Emily were out of earshot before she zipped up her parka and said, "Well, now I feel like total crap. She thinks we're being kind to her! We don't tell her that her mum is dead and we get her out of her own house purely so we can break into it and snoop. It's all wrong!"

"But you noticed it? When Bethan said that Emily's

mum wouldn't want her to be upset. All the weird stuff stopped, instantly," said Hashim. "That means Emily's mum was definitely here. That means she goes where Emily goes, which means she's gone home with Bethan. Probably. I'd text her, but my phone's still dead."

"If it was Emily's mum who helped me and Bethan get away from Carter, she wasn't with Emily then," Kelly reminded Hashim. "But anyway, this detective stuff is crap. We have to tell her what we know, and the only thing we know is that her mum is probably dead."

"You heard what Grandad said," Jay reminded her as they headed across town. "He said Emily probably already knows what's happened and that we just need to help her to remember. If we crash in now, and tell her that her mum is not only dead but an unhappy ghost, she might never get over it."

"She's never going to get over it anyway," Kelly assured him.

"Look, you don't know what's happened to your mum." Jay stopped dead in his tracks, putting his hand on Kelly's shoulder. "Would you like to be told flat out that she's dead? Would you really want to know that?"

"Too harsh, man," Hashim frowned. "Lay off."

"Well, would you?" Jay pressed Kelly. "Because we've got to tell Emily the truth sooner or later, and all I'm trying to do is find the best way. Is it so bad that she gets one more night before knowing that her mother is never coming back?"

Kelly shook Jay's hand from her shoulder and marched off. "Come on," she said. "Let's get this over with."

CHAP✝ER FOUR✝EEN

"Wow, you really like black," Emily said, looking around Bethan's room which was indeed painted black, much to her mother's regret. She also had a black duvet and a black rug that covered up most of the hideous patterned carpet, and some dark purple curtains that she'd found in Oxfam.

"Yeah, I know," Bethan said. "I used to think it was cool, but, I don't know, recently it all seems a bit... depressing."

"Mum painted my room pink – but hot pink, you know? She says a person needs a bit of colour in their life, living in this town." Emily pulled back the curtains and gazed out across the estate, the darkness spangled with hundreds of lit windows.

"She's right," Bethan said. "Every summer we go and stay in my uncle Jim's caravan in Wales. It's fully lame and gross and I can't stand it, but Mum says I have to go until I'm at least sixteen, which is so unfair… But the thing is, it's really different in Wales. It's like the sky is lighter, the air is fresher and… you never get the feeling that there's something waiting in the shadows. And I don't think it's just Wales. I think that most other places apart from Woodsville are like that too. I mean, I've heard other people call their town 'dead', but I don't think anywhere is quite as dead as Woodsville."

"We want to pack up and leave," Emily smiled, her eyes brightening at the thought. "Mum is always talking about it, going off somewhere, anywhere. She says that one of these days, we'll just get on a plane and go anywhere sunny. She hates Woodsville as much as me. Weirdsville she calls it, you know, like the column in the newspaper? I'd love to leave here, but I get the feeling that I can't. Do you know what I mean? I get the feeling I'll always be stuck here."

"I totally know what you mean. You hate school even more than me, don't you?" Bethan asked as she flicked through her collection of DVDs, looking for something fun and light-hearted. Suddenly her obsession with horror films didn't seem quite so appropriate. "Our school is such an utter waste of time and all the other kids are totally pointless." Bethan paused, thinking about her fledgling relationships with Jay, Kelly and Hashim. "Well, almost all of them. But you look like every minute you have to spend there might actually kill you."

"I feel like that," Emily nodded. "Everyone hates me. I don't know why. I never say anything bad about anyone, or try to hurt anyone. I spend all my time trying not to get noticed, but the more I do that, the more everyone wants to attack me, even the teachers."

"Maybe it's because we're all scared," Bethan said thoughtfully. "When you're scared, sometimes it helps to find a person weaker than you to make yourself feel strong. They see that you're frightened and they pounce. Look at Kelly. There's no one scarier than Kelly, but there's no one more scared either. She's got to live with the fact that there's someone out there who really wants to hurt her. And not just steal her iPod and rough her up a bit. I mean hurt her, put her in hospital at the very least."

"This is such a horrible place," Emily blurted out suddenly. "I hate it! I'd do anything to leave… I just want my mum!"

"I know," Bethan said, unable to look Emily in the eye. She held up a DVD about cheerleaders that her mum had bought her for Christmas and that she'd thrown in the bin in disgust. Her mum must have fished it out again and hidden it among her collection; for once, Bethan was glad of parental interference. "Come on, let's watch this rubbish."

*   *   *

"I thought you said this would be easy," Jay whispered as Kelly tried once more to open Emily's front door with the Tesco Club Card that Jay had borrowed from his mum's purse on the way out.

"Just shut up and make sure no one sees me," Kelly hissed as she jiggled the plastic between the lock and the door frame. "It takes a bit of practice and, funnily enough, I'm not in the habit of breaking into people's houses."

"Just get a move on," Hashim said, looking up at the dark house. "Let's just get in and out, and get this over with."

"It's a total waste of time anyway," Kelly grumbled. "What do you think we're going to find in there – a signed confession from Emily admitting to topping her mum? A map to show where she's buried the body?"

"If we ever get in, we'll find *something*. Grandad said…"

"Your bloody grandad is one step from senile," Kelly said, taking the card out of the door and leaning her back against it. "Encouraging his grandson to break and enter, does that tell you noth— Oh!"

Kelly stumbled backwards as the front door swung open, Jay's arm around her waist stopped her fall.

"You did it!" Hashim seemed impressed.

"No way," frowned Kelly.

"You must have loosened it," Jay said, looking into her eyes, his heart pounding.

"Must have." Awkwardly, Kelly shrugged and righted herself, pushing Jay's arm away as she regained her balance. "Anyway, I think I've broken your mum's card."

"Come on, let's get inside." Hashim barged past, glad to be off the street which for some reason he found much more menacing than Emily's haunted house. He tried the light switch by the door. "No electric again." He checked under the stairs. "And the emergency supply is all used up."

"You mean Emily's been living with no leccy since the weekend?" Kelly asked. "And none of us checked on her. That's awful."

"That's weird," Jay said. "One girl, living on her own – the emergency supply should have lasted a lot longer than a few days."

"Which shows just how very little you know about girls," Kelly grinned. "Telly, radio, iPod charger, laptop, straighteners, curlers. Mobile charger…"

"Yes, *girls*, but we're not talking about girls. We talking about Emily. I think it's got something to do with her mum. Ghosts need energy to manifest. She probably drains off electricity whenever she's around – think of the light bulb flickering back at mine and all our phones going dead. I think it's the same thing. Did anyone bring a torch?"

"Better than that," Hashim said. "I thought this might

happen, so I got this at that newsagent's we stopped at for crisps." He produced a token and, ducking under the stairs, slipped it into the meter. The house was suddenly flooded with light and noise, the TV and radio on full blast.

"So you reckon it's the ghost draining the energy then," Kelly yelled over the din as she stomped into the front room to kill the TV. "God, no wonder she goes through tokens so quick. Everything in the house is on again."

"Maybe her mum's ghost does it – remember Emily said she liked the place to be full of noise."

"Or maybe Emily's just trying not to feel so alone," said Hashim.

"Yeah, let's not start assuming *everything* is paranormal," Kelly agreed. "Let's just assume that Emily isn't that fussed about her carbon footprint."

"We'll have to take it out when we go though," Jay said. "Otherwise she'll know we've been here."

"We can't just leave her in the dark," Kelly protested.

"And anyway, we can't take it out," Hashim added slowly. "Once it's in, it's in."

"Oh great, so she'll know someone's been here!" Jay clapped his hand against his forehead. "Brilliant."

"Look. Emily's living in a house where she can go to sleep in one room and wake up in another. Do you really think the power being back on is going to freak her out all that much? Now let's gets on with it, all right? If we've got to turn over Emily's house, let's do it without the chatting."

"Fine," said Jay. "Let's split up and look round."

Hashim and Kelly looked at each other, remembering that face on the monitor.

"*Or* let's all look around together?" Hashim suggested. After peering up the staircase for a second, Jay didn't protest.

They went into the living room first. Kelly walked across the room and looked around. "I still don't know what we're looking for," she said. "I mean, what do we expect to find?"

"Anything that might tell us something about Emily's mum." Jay studied an ornament-filled, dusty mantel that ran over the electric coal-effect fire and suddenly snatched up a photo in a frame.

"It's Emily and her mum," Hashim said. "Her mum looks a lot more… alive there than in the video."

"So what does that tell us?" Kelly asked. "Apart from the fact that ghosts tend not to look their best, what with being dead and everything?"

"Well, they're leaning on a car, a blue Ford Fiesta. It looks like their car. But there's no Ford Fiesta parked outside the house, which probably means that whenever Emily's mum left, she went in that car."

"But why didn't she tell Emily? Why has Emily never mentioned the car? And if her mum did leave in the car, what happened to her after she left... what killed her?" Kelly asked. "The photo doesn't tell us anything we really need to know; it just makes a whole load more questions."

Kelly's head snapped up and she looked around the empty room. "Look, you'd save us all a lot of time if you'd just turn up now and tell us what happened," she challenged nothing in particular. "Any chance of that?"

Jay and Hashim held their breath, but the house remained silent.

"Exactly. Typical bloody ghost," Kelly complained. "Can't just tip up and tell us stuff, has to be all mysterious and difficult. I think it's attention-seeking myself. I think if you can manifest and move stuff and walk through walls, you could send a nice clear and detailed e-mail, for example, or maybe a text. It's just grandstanding, that's what it is." She scowled into thin air. "Bet you could, couldn't you – if you tried?"

"Right, well, can we just skip the invoking of the dead and move on?" said Jay. "Cos I don't mind if Mrs Night prefers to leave us to work it out from the clues myself."

"Nope, I don't have a problem with that *at all,*" Hashim added.

"Come on then, you pair of girls," Kelly sighed.

The kitchen was exactly as they had left it on Friday. Even the cup of black tea that they had made Emily was still on the table, dust settling on its filmy surface.

"Still the same half bottle of milk, only a bit more off," Kelly said as she opened the fridge door. "She can't eat anything in here."

"Well, she probably doesn't," said Jay. "Especially if there's no electric. She probably goes and gets a sandwich or something. I know I would. Cook anything in this kitchen and it would probably kill you."

"Anything else, apart from the fact that Emily doesn't like washing up?" Hashim asked, peering into a fetid sink. The three of them looked around the kitchen.

"Hold on... what's that?" Kelly spotted a piece of paper sticking out from behind a jar on a shelf. She retrieved it and blew away a thin layer of dust.

"E-tickets. Two flights to Spain for April. One-way tickets. Emily and her mum were going away, and by the look of these tickets, it doesn't look like they were planning on coming back." Kelly examined the piece of paper more closely. "Emily said her mum's been missing since New Year's Day. These tickets were *booked* on New Year's Day!"

"But Emily's never mentioned that they were planning a holiday."

"Maybe she didn't know. Perhaps it was supposed to be a surprise," Kelly suggested.

"Or maybe it's like Grandad said. Maybe she forgot all about it because it happened on a day that her brain doesn't *want* to remember."

"So we know two things. Emily's mum had a car which doesn't seem to be around, and they were leaving Woodsville, which either Emily didn't know about or has forgotten..." Jay mused.

"That's it! I've worked it out!" Kelly yelled.

"Have you?" Jay asked, full of admiration.

"No, of course I haven't, idiot. So we know the travel arrangements. Now let's check upstairs where maybe we'll find a corpse or a murder weapon or something more useful."

Upstairs was also exactly as they'd left it. Kelly led the way into Emily's small bedroom, looking around and trying to relate what she saw there to the girl that she had begun to get to know.

The room was painted a surprisingly bright pink and it was covered with paintings, all of which were signed by Emily, all of places that couldn't be anywhere near Woodsville. There were scenes of the sea, a blue sky and fields filled with a million different-coloured flowers. Kelly opened Emily's wardrobe. Just like her mother, Emily seemed to have an entirely different taste in clothes from what Kelly saw at school, where Emily dressed more like one of the shadows that she hoped to blend into. There were pretty tops, flowery dresses and a small collection of brightly-coloured sandals.

"We don't know Emily at all, do we?" Hashim said,

looking over Kelly's shoulder as she fingered a red summer dress. "It's like she has another life outside of school, like when she's here with her mum she happy and creative and… herself, I guess. All this time she'd been hiding from us, from everyone."

"Well, school can be a pretty harsh place, especially if you don't fit in," Jay said.

"It's not as if any of us bothered even trying to get to know her," said Kelly thoughtfully. "We don't even know each other."

The three were silent for a moment, each of them considering exactly what had changed since they had decided to help Emily.

"Well, I can't see any clues in here," Jay said after a moment.

"Except that, unlike the rest of the house, Emily keeps her room tidy, like her mum's. Look, she's even made her bed."

"We should check her mum's room too," said Jay, looking down the corridor.

"Really?" Hashim asked him. "Couldn't we just skip that bit and, you know, leave?"

"Maybe we could," Jay said. "After all, we've investigated that room before so…"

As he spoke, the handle on Mrs Night's bedroom door turned and the door opened, just a few centimetres.

"Finally, some action," Kelly breathed.

"We could pretend that never happened," whispered Hashim.

"We could," Jay agreed. "We could run right past that open door without looking inside and it would probably be fine."

At that instant, all of the lights in the house went off except for the one in Emily's mum's bedroom. A shadow flickered across the wedge of light behind the doorway.

"Oh God, we have to look." Kelly clutched Jay's hand without realising it until he squeezed her fingers back. "This is what we came for. She's here. She's talking to us."

"I was hoping she'd talk to us with the lights on," Jay hissed, but he didn't let go of Kelly's hand.

"Come on." Hashim took a breath. "I'll go first."

Taking a deep breath, he grabbed Kelly's other hand and led the way.

The TV and DVD packed up fifteen minutes before the end of the film.

"What the...?" Bethan moaned, before sitting bolt upright from where she had been leaning on a beanbag on the floor and looking around the room. The room didn't feel any different – it wasn't colder or darker – but Emily was no longer lying on the bed.

"Emily?" Bethan stood up and switched on the overhead

light. "Em, where are you?" She opened her bedroom door and found Emily walking up the hallway.

"Sorry, I just went to the loo," Emily smiled.

"I didn't hear you go." Bethan pressed her hand to her chest where she could feel her heart thumping against her ribs.

"I think you were a bit into that blonde girl suddenly getting together with the baseball guy to notice, you old romantic," Emily teased.

"I know!" Bethan laughed. "I got totally sucked in by it. This is what I'm always saying. The world doesn't want us to know anything; it just wants us to watch slushy chick flicks, believe that everything will turn out OK and stay in line until we've got our drudge of a dead-end job and are just another ghost in the machine, making the wheels go round and round until we die."

"I have no idea what you just said," said Emily.

"Well, we can't see the end of the film anyway," Bethan said. "Telly's conked out. How about a hot chocolate and then we can guess the ending? I think the cheerleader went psycho and took a chainsaw to all the others. How about you?"

Emily's smiled faded a little. "Actually, I'm tired and it's late. I think I'll go home."

"No, don't." Bethan tried to stall her. She had no way of knowing whether the others had left Emily's house or not. Bethan had recharged her own phone, but she assumed that the others' would still be flat, which meant they wouldn't be able to tell her when the coast was clear. "Mum and Dad are at work and I hate being here on my own. You can sleep over if you like?"

"Thanks, but I want to sleep at home. You know, just in case. What if Mum turned up and I wasn't there? Think how she'd worry."

"I suppose," Bethan said in dismay. "But Emily, it's late. You shouldn't be walking across the estate on your own. Anything could happen. I know, I'll walk with you."

"Then you'd just have to walk back on your own. Look, Bethan, I'll be fine. No one is going to mug me. Do I look like I've got anything worth taking?"

"I guess not," Bethan said. "But you'll be at school tomorrow, right? It's photo day – you can't miss that!"

"Are you joking?" Emily asked her. "I'd have thought that was your least favourite thing."

"It is normally," Bethan said. "But this year... well, there are actually some people I don't mind standing next to. And you're one of them. You're a cool girl, Emily. I'm sorry I didn't find that out until now."

"Really?" Emily asked as Bethan walked her to the door.

"Yes, really. I've really enjoyed this evening." And it was true. For most of the evening, Bethan had completely forgotten that the main reason she had invited Emily round was to get her out of the house. For most of the evening, she'd just had a good time.

She watched as Emily disappeared into the thicket of darkness that collected at the end of the corridor. She waited until she heard the ping of the lift and then she closed the front door and double-locked it.

Bethan just prayed that Jay and the others would be out of Emily's house before she got back because she'd hate it if Emily thought this evening had only been about getting her out of there. Quite unexpectedly, Bethan had made another friend and she didn't want to hurt her.

His mouth dry, Hashim pushed open the bedroom door with his free hand. He'd expected the room to be freezing and full of anger, just like Jay's had been a few hours ago, but the first thing that hit him was a wave of heat.

"It's boiling in here," he said, unzipping his jacket as beads of sweat broke out on his top lip. He dropped Kelly's hand and walked into the room. He didn't know what he'd been expecting, the ghost of Emily's mother suspended in mid-air, shrieking like a banshee probably, but the room, although oppressively hot, appeared to be empty.

"There's that scent again," Kelly said, her nose wrinkling as she sniffed the air. "That's Mrs Night's perfume from the green bottle. This room is filled with it."

The three ventured into the centre of the room, standing

shoulder to shoulder as if at any minute they might need to defend themselves against an unseen visitor.

"That heater is on full blast." Jay nodded at the unit against the wall. "That'll make the tokens run out quick."

"But this is the only room in the house with the heating switched on," Hashim said. "The room that no one's using right now. Or at least, no one we can see."

"This is different," Kelly said as she realised that she still had Jay's hand in hers. Reluctantly, she let go of his fingers. "This room doesn't feel frightening, or angry and confused. This room feels full of… love."

Kelly swallowed as a single tear tracked down her cheek. "This room is full of a mother's love for her daughter," she said, stifling a sob as she was suddenly overwhelmed with longing for her own mother. "You need to help us," Kelly pleaded, talking into the warm air. "You need to tell us what to do."

They heard a thin, high-pitched squeak from behind, like fingers being scraped across a blackboard. As one, they slowly turned towards the sound.

In the thick condensation that filmed the bedroom window, a finger-thick line was being drawn by an unseen hand. Silently, they stood transfixed as they watched the message finally form: *Help her*.

As the last curve on the "r" was completed, the room plunged into darkness. The oppressive heat instantly chilled, leaving the house empty, silent and dark once more, as if it had been sucked dry.

"Can we go now, please?" Hashim whispered.

Jay had already started down the stairs.

CHAPTER FIFTEEN

"All I'm saying," Kelly said, "is that now we have to tell her everything. And I mean *everything*. We have to show her the video; we have to tell we were at her house; we have to tell her about the message." She was applying lipgloss as they stood with the rest of their class on the playground, waiting for the photographer to be ready, accomplishing a feat in multitasking that neither Jay nor Hashim could take their eyes off.

"Yeah, but how do you tell a person that?" Jay asked.

"And where is she anyway?" Bethan looked around. "She said she'd be here. I hope she got home OK. Emily must be the only fifteen-year-old in the Western hemisphere not to have a mobile."

"Maybe she decided to give the photo a miss," Jay said. "Seriously, why do they make us do this every year?"

"Because I get better looking every year, that's why," Hashim grinned. "It'd be a crime not to record it."

"That message on the window – it sounded like a warning to me," Kelly went on. "Maybe someone's out to get Emily and that's what her mum is so worried about. Maybe her mum got herself into trouble, like Mandy Harris in the next tower. She borrowed five hundred quid off a loan shark to take her kids on holiday, but by the time she got back he said she owed him five grand and she ended up with her flat trashed and five broken fingers. And she still owes him. By the time she's paid him off she'll be a hundred and seven." Her face fell as she remembered her own problems. "Or maybe it's someone like Carter."

"Have you had any more trouble from Carter?" asked Jay, resisting the urge to put a protective arm around her.

"Not since the lift," Kelly shrugged. "I don't know. I feel sort of safe right now. Like whatever it was that day is looking out for me."

"Yeah, but if that was Emily's mum then why can't she protect Emily too?" Hashim put in.

"I don't know," Kelly said. "I'm just saying, if it was something like that, then that could be why she booked those one-way flights to Spain, to get away from some kind of danger. But maybe whoever they were running from got to Emily's mum first, and now she's worried they're going after Emily."

"That's a lot of maybes," Hashim said, running his fingers through his hair. "How do I look, girls? Fittest lad in the class photo or what?"

"What," Bethan and Kelly said in unison.

"Kelly's right. I don't think we have a choice any more." Bethan scanned the milling crowd for Emily. "Think about it – her mum is dead. Which means her body is somewhere waiting to be found. It's possible that Emily is in danger and has no idea, and we haven't got a clue either. All we can guess is that the ghost of her mum won't rest until Emily's safe. And the only person who'll know anything new now is Emily. We have to tell her everything and get her to remember. It's the only way we're going to sort this."

"It's just... *how*?" Jay shrugged. "I mean, look at us. We're just a bunch of kids who think we've seen some weird stuff. Are we sure this isn't just us winding ourselves up, seeing things that aren't there? In New England in the seventeenth century, whole communities got swept up into believing that anyone who was a bit different was a witch. Hundreds of totally innocent people were tried. Dozens were hung and even burnt. But it was mass hysteria. It was all a mistake."

"You said the video footage couldn't be faked, or an accident," Kelly reminded him.

"It can't, not that I can see. But I'm a fifteen-year-old geek. I don't *know*."

"At least he admits he's a geek," said Hashim.

"Your grandad told us to break into her house and search for clues!" Bethan exclaimed.

"I know, but Grandad's a bit off the wall," Jay said. "I love him and everything, but… what if he's just a bit mental?"

"We all saw the message on the window."

"We all *thought* we saw the message on the window. In the Second World War, hundreds of merchant seamen thought they saw the faces of two dead comrades floating in the water behind the ship for two days. Maybe they did. Or maybe it was auto-suggestion. One person believes they see something, then everyone else falls into line because no one wants to be the odd one out. Which is more likely?"

"So what about the things I can see then?" Hashim said, suddenly serious. "Like the kid smoking under that tree, in flares and a biker jacket, with a knife gash from ear to ear that makes him look like his head should fall off at any minute. That's not mass hysteria. And if he's not a ghost then he's got some serious health issues."

"RIGHT, YOU LOT, GET INTO YOUR LINES NOW! I HAVEN'T GOT ALL DAY!" Mr Bacon bellowed, and they jostled with everyone, keen to be in the back row.

"I know," Jay said as they clambered up on to the bench that elevated them above the rest. "And I know this is Weirdsville where anything can happen and probably will.

It's just – don't we want to be sure that we've got it right before we tell Emily we think her mother is dead? For Emily's sake?"

"OK, kids, look into the lens and smile." The photographer tried valiantly to make himself heard over the rabble.

"We have to tell her what we think we know," Kelly said decisively. "We'll show her what we've found out and we'll let her decide."

"Kelly's right, we have to tell Emily as soon as possible."

"Tell me what?" came Emily's quiet voice. The thin girl smiled slightly as she squeezed herself into a space between Kelly and Bethan.

"And smile… Oh, what the—? Sorry, kids, battery's died. It'll take me two secs to get another one in." The photographer bent down to rifle in his equipment bag and the three lines immediately descended into chaos.

"Next idiot to make a sound gets detention for a week!" Mr Bacon warned them.

"We think we've found out some stuff, about your mum," Kelly said. "But we're not really sure and we might be wrong and what we think we know is pretty—"

"One. More. Word. King!" Mr Bacon pointed at Kelly.

"Talk after," Jay whispered out of the corner of his mouth.

Emily nodded, the smile she had arrived with fading into a frown.

"And say cheese!" the photographer yelled.

Thirty teenagers shouted an awful lot of words out. None of them was cheese.

Jay watched Emily's face as he closed his laptop. They had gone to the old history block after the photo shoot was finished, using the chaos of a class desperate to be anywhere but there as cover. Whether they'd all get away with missing double maths was another thing, but at that moment it was the least of their worries.

"Is that your mum, Emily?" Kelly asked gently, covering the other girl's hand with her own. It was as cold as ice.

"Yes," Emily whispered. "That's Mum. And you captured that the night we did the investigation?"

"Yes," Jay said awkwardly, feeling somehow responsible for the pain now etched across Emily's face.

"Then she's dead."

"Well, we don't know that for sure—" Jay began, but Bethan stopped him with a look.

"Jay, let's just tell her everything we know."

Emily listened quietly as Kelly and Bethan told her about what happened at the lift and how they thought it must have been Emily's mum that had helped them. Then Hashim told her about the people he saw, the people that he believed were ghosts, and finally, Jay told her about the visit to her house the night before, when she'd been with Bethan.

"You broke into my house?" Emily exclaimed. "To snoop on me? I thought we were friends."

"We are friends, honestly," Kelly reassured her. "We're trying to help you. We only went round because, well, you seem so muddled about what happened on the day your mum went missing. We thought maybe you just couldn't remember. We were trying to find some clues, something that might help us find out what happened. And we didn't break in, not exactly. The house sort of let us in."

Emily looked at Bethan, her eyes dark and burning with the heat of unshed tears. "And you invited me over just to get me out of the way?"

"No, no," Bethan said. "I mean, yes, OK, it was at first. But Emily, I had fun with you. I really did. I like you."

"We all do," Hashim said. "And we don't want to see you hurt, right? This started out as a bit of a joke, but things have got dark round here. We really want to help you."

Emily nodded, removing her slender hand from under Kelly's and folding it tightly within her skirt.

"So what did you find out?" she asked, her voice scarcely more than a whisper.

Jay and Hashim exchanged glances.

"We saw the photo of you and your mum standing next to a car. A blue Ford Fiesta. Well, it's not parked near your house. So where is it, Emily?"

"The car!" Emily looked surprised. "I'd forgotten about the car... why would I do that?"

"Well, was your mum driving it on the day she went missing?" Hashim asked.

Emily frowned. "She must have been. She loved that car. Had a name for it and everything..." Emily trailed off, staring into the distance as if she were trying really hard to bring a faraway picture into focus.

"What about these?" Jay flattened the e-tickets out on the dusty desk and pushed them towards Emily. Without touching them, her eyes scanned the print.

"Spain?" she said.

"Do you think it was a surprise?" Hashim prompted her. "Do you think your mum was planning a surprise trip? Cos look, they were booked on New Year's Day, for April."

"No." Emily shook her head and closed her eyes. "No, it wasn't a surprise. Mum told me. We were going away, just like she'd always promised. She said she had a Christmas bonus and she decided we needed a treat." Emily's eyes filled with fear. "Why didn't I remember that?"

"Did you know the tickets were one-way?" Kelly asked her. "Do you know if you were planning to come back?"

"One-way?" Emily looked lost. "I don't know. I can't make myself remember – what's wrong with me?"

"Nothing," Kelly reassured her. "Look, we think that

223

whatever happened to your mum, you probably know already. But that you find it too hard to think about, so your brain's made you forget."

Emily looked at her. "I'm frightened, Kelly."

"Me too," Kelly told her. "I'm frightened every day. I think if I could block out the things that scared me and act as if they'd never happened then I would. And I think... I think you have to be frightened before you can be brave. But the thing is, Emily, you need to know what happened to your mum, and she needs you to know and... there is one other thing."

Kelly looked up at Jay, who looked at Hashim, who looked at his feet.

"What?" Emily asked, her voice hoarse with anxiety.

Kelly felt as if suddenly all the air had been sucked out of the room, despite the broken windows. No one wanted to tell Emily, but somebody had to.

"Your mum left you a message," Kelly said.

"I need to go home," Emily said, as if Kelly hadn't just told her what had been written on the window. "I'm tired. I need to go."

"You can't just go. We think you're in danger, Emily. And your mum is trying her best to warn you. You have to listen."

"But that's just stupid. I'm not in danger. Mum never

had any enemies. Everybody liked her. She wasn't like me – she was popular. She got on with people. Nobody would have ever wanted to hurt her. She was like a ray of sunshine – even on that day when it was cold and raining and miserable, she knew exactly how to cheer us up…" Emily stalled as a memory came back to her. "She said we should go shopping, check out the sales and buy some things for our holiday. I've just remembered – that's what we did that day she went missing. We went shopping."

"And what else?" Jay pressed her. "What else happened that day?"

"I don't know." Emily's face seemed to be folding inwards. "Why can't I remember?"

"You can," Bethan reassured her. "You just remembered something then. It's slowly coming back to you, Em."

"I don't remember anything else though, except waking up at home and knowing Mum wasn't there."

"Well, whatever happened it's somewhere in there," Hashim said, gently tapping Emily's head. "And even though it's scary and difficult, it needs to come out."

"But how?" Emily asked, her complexion shifting from grey to white, as if the worry was draining every ounce of colour from her.

"You remember leaving home with your mum that morning to go shopping," Jay said. "We need to jog your memory. We should recreate that day. Do exactly what you and your mum did. Tomorrow. We'll come to your house and then… go shopping. What time did you go out?"

"After lunch – but I don't remember what else happened…" Emily sounded uncertain.

"Not yet, but you might."

"We'll be bunking school," Bethan pointed out, because as much as she liked to come across as a rebel, the idea of missing a whole day gave her a tight little knot in her belly.

"There's always a plus," said Hashim.

"So what? Nothing ever happens anyway, and its only for the afternoon," Kelly said. "And this is important."

"So we'll come round yours then," Jay said. "Two-ish OK?"

Emily nodded. "But what if nothing comes back to me? What then?"

"Then I guess we won't have any choice," Jay said. "We'll have to ask for help."

"Which means the police and social services." Emily looked at her tightly knotted hands. "I've got to go. I'll see you tomorrow."

"Aren't you going back to class?" Bethan asked as Emily hurried towards the door.

"No, I'm tired. I want to go home."

"I'll walk with you," Kelly offered.

"I want to be on my own."

After Emily had gone the others looked at each other.

"Are we sure we know what we're doing?" Bethan spoke first. "What if we end up hurting her even more?"

"You saw how frightened she is," Jay said. "She looked like she was about to throw herself under a bus. And more than that, who's going to believe that her mum's been haunting her? If she tells that to some busybody from the council, she'll end up in psychiatric ward or worse."

"We could show them the video, tell them all the stuff that's happened."

"There are thousands of video clips all over the internet supposedly showing ghosts. OK, we know it's not a hoax, but we can't prove it isn't." Jay ran his fingers through his hair. "None of us knew what we were getting into when we started this. But we're in it now and I think that tomorrow will be our last chance to finish it. And if we can't, God knows what will happen to Emily."

There was silence as each of them considered what exactly that might be.

"Hang on a minute," Hashim said. "Emily believes her mum is dead, thinks she's going to end up in care and we've just told her about a message from beyond the grave warning her that someone is out to get her. What if she *does* throw herself under a bus? What if she tries to—"

"We've got to go after her!"

They all scrambled out of the building, grabbing bags and coats as they fled, pounding towards the school gates.

"She can't have gone far," Hashim shouted as he raced up the road, by far the fittest of the four. He skidded to a halt at the corner, searching for a glimpse of Emily.

"Which way would she have gone?" he asked the others as they joined him, Jay out of breath and Kelly struggling to keep up in her heels.

"That's the quickest way back to the old town." Kelly nodded down a long, straight avenue.

"She could have gone anywhere," Bethan said. "She could be anywhere in Woodsville."

"Well, she said she was going home," Jay reminded them. "We might as well go there."

Emily's house was quiet and dark when they arrived. They rang the bell and knocked but there was no answer.

"Try the door," Kelly suggested. "You never know – maybe it'll let us in like last time."

First Jay and then Hashim tried the door. Jay jiggled the lock, then Hashim shrugged his jacket off and charged it. "Flipping OW!" he yelled, clutching his shoulder as the door remained unmoved.

"That's what you get for showing off." Bethan couldn't help smiling.

"That door's not budging today," Hashim said. "I swear,

it's even more solid than when we were trying to break in. It's almost like there's something on the other side keeping it shut."

"Well, if Emily's in there, then I think she must be OK," said Kelly. "If she wasn't, her mum would let us in, like before. She wants us to protect Emily. And if she's not in there, well, she could be anywhere. There's nothing we can do until tomorrow, when we meet her."

Reluctantly, they turned on their heels and began heading back to the estate, Hashim tagging along because he didn't want to be on his own, which the others knew even if he didn't admit it.

The bond between them was growing stronger than any of them realised. And with it came a sense of purpose, even a sense of destiny. Each step was taking them deeper into a journey from which there was no return, and in the morning they would find out exactly what that meant.

CHAP✝ER SIX✝EEN

As Kelly sneaked out of school to meet the others the next afternoon, she was trying to remember what the weather was like on New Year's Day. Chances were that it had been exactly like today, cold and damp with the clouds lying low in the sky, as if they might catch and scrape on the jagged tops of the tower blocks. Skies were rarely blue in Woodsville. Even in the middle of summer, when the air was so hot and sticky that it felt like every breath you took was mixed with glue, the sky was hardly ever cloudless.

Woodsville and its surroundings had special weather. Kelly half remembered hearing about it in geography. Like Wales was famous for rain and Scotland was famous for being cold, something about Woodsville made it a bit like living in the middle of a rainforest. Even though they'd ripped down the forest to build the town decades ago, when a load of scientists had come to check out global warming, or whatever, in the area, they'd discovered that the climate was that of the dense and ancient forest which had once covered the town. "Ghost Tree Effect" the boffins had called it, and someone had even made a documentary, which got repeated every now and again on the National Geographic channel. Not that it made any difference to the people who lived and worked in Woodsville. They grew up not expecting a blue sky, so when one never appeared, no one was disappointed.

Anyway, if the weather, or the chill in the air, or the damp on her skin were needed to help Emily remember that day, then she had nothing to worry about. It was perfect traumatic-memory-jogging weather.

Thrusting her hands deeper into her parka pockets, Kelly turned a corner heading towards the bus stop where she'd agreed to meet the others, and came face to face with Carter.

"Oh." She breathed the word, barely audible over the blood that was suddenly thundering in her ears as her heart made an attempt to escape through her ribcage. Bracing herself, Kelly closed her eyes and for a second wondered if she would be able to bear the pain of what was about to happen, or if she would cry and scream and beg for mercy. Finally, she wondered if she would ever open her eyes again.

When she felt and heard nothing, Kelly assumed that she must be dead. That Carter had killed her and been mercifully quick about it. Opening her eyes again, she realised that either the afterlife was disappointingly like the one she'd just left or nothing had yet happened. Kelly made herself look Carter in the face and realised that the latter was true. He was standing there, staring at her... and *he* looked afraid.

"Well, go on then," Kelly said, surprised by the irritation in her voice. "Get it over with, will you? I can't stand this any more, Carter. Just do whatever you've got planned."

Carter shook his head. "I ain't gonna touch you and you know it," he told her, glancing around as if he were afraid to be alone with her.

"You're... What you on about?"

Carter shook his head, looking down at his trainers. "I don't know what weird witchy stuff you've pulled, Kelly King, but whatever it is, it's worked. I can't take it no more. I was coming to tell you it's over. You've won. I'm not coming after you any more. I can't sleep, I can't even close my eyes... I'll tell the lads that we're going after something bigger. You ain't worth it. And you... well, you don't tell no one, will you. If this got out, I'd be nothing round here."

"*What?*"

"I know, I know I ain't got any right to ask after what

I've done, but... please, Kelly. Respect – it's all I've got."

Kelly stared at him, amazed to see his complexion pale and feet shift in discomfort under her scrutiny. What she had to concentrate on was that Carter was letting her off the hook. He was telling her that he wasn't coming after her any more. If she asked him what he was on about, he'd realise that whatever power he imagined she had over him didn't exist. Kelly had absolutely no idea what she could have possibly done that had changed his mind, and she didn't care. The only thing to do was to keep her mouth shut and look like she could shrivel him with a single glance. That at least was something Kelly knew how to do.

"Keep your gang off my landing and you've got a deal," Kelly told him coldly.

"Done." Carter did not raise his head to look at her. "And you'll stop the screaming, screaming in my head? Because ever since that first night it happened, when I was out with the dog, it don't stop. I've tried to block it out and get on with things, but it goes on and on, all night, Kelly. All night telling me to help her, over and over again. I can't take much more. I feel like I'm going mad."

"Help her?" Kelly thought of the message scrawled on the window in Emily's house.

"Yeah, help her – help you."

"Me?" Kelly asked him. "How do you know this voice is telling you to help me?"

"Because I see your face whenever I hear it, like its you that's screaming and in all this pain, but it's me that feels it. It's me that feels the pain. I don't know, maybe I'm going mental, but either way I'm finished with you." Carter glanced around the empty street. "See? I'm helping her, OK? OK?" He looked back at Kelly who looked into his hollow eyes. Carter had been getting the same message as they had got for Emily – but why? Unless… unless that message wasn't meant for Emily at all.

Kelly felt a sudden chill freeze her to the core.

"Right then. Well, I've got places to be," she said, quickly walking past him, hoping to keep herself from folding into a gibbering wreck at least until he was out of sight.

But he called after her. "Kelly!" Taking a breath, she slowly turned and looked at him. "And you'll make it stop now, yeah? Please. I've helped you now, haven't I?"

Kelly paused. "Might do." Then she turned her back on Carter and got out of his sight as fast as her heels would take her.

"Emily, you're here," Hashim said, finding the girl waiting on her doorstep. He was the first to arrive. "Didn't see you in school this morning."

"I think I forgot to go," Emily said. "Anyway, I'm

ready. I've got to do this, whether I like it or not. So here I am."

"We were worried about you yesterday – you looked so upset. We came round to check on you, but there was no answer."

"Did you?" Emily's smile warmed her face and Hashim could see a glimpse of a pretty girl hiding underneath the curtain of hair.

"Yeah. Did you go out for a walk or something?"

"No, I was here. I must have been asleep. I was dead tired. I'm sorry."

"Don't be." Hashim looked down the road and saw the others approaching. Bethan and Jay were listening to Kelly talking animatedly about something, her arms flailing about as if words weren't enough to describe what she was saying.

"I'm telling you, he stood there like a little kid who was scared to look under his bed and he begged me to make it stop and he said he kept hearing this warning over and over again, 'help her', just like what was written on the window. What do you think that means? What could be more scary than Carter?"

"I don't know, but if it's on your side, it has to be a good thing, right?" Bethan replied. "If it means you don't have to go around looking over your shoulder all the time. We assumed it was Emily's ghost that helped us in the lift that day, but maybe it was yours. I mean, let's face it. Weirdsville is obviously packed with them."

Kelly paused for a moment. "My ghost," she said slowly, lowering her voice. "You mean – my mum?"

"No, no," Jay reassured her. "It doesn't have to be your mum. It could be another relation, your gran maybe – or something else entirely. But whatever it is, it's on your side. You don't have to be scared."

"You're right," Kelly said slowly. "I thought something was after *me*, something spooky – but that's not how it is. The spooky thing was on my side. The spooky thing helped me by scaring the life out of Carter. The spooky thing is cool!"

Hashim took a second to enjoy Kelly's smile. Full of genuine joy, it lit her face from within, like a candle in a paper lantern. He'd always thought Kelly was fit in a scary sort of way. He'd never realised that she was actually beautiful until now, seeing her frown and laugh and smile, like she was really happy.

"Em, you're OK!" Kelly beamed. "Did Hashim tell you he was trying to bash down your door yesterday?"

"Er, not exactly." Emily smiled. "Shall we go? I know we're trying to recreate that day, but we can't drive so I thought we'd get the bus."

"Hang on," Jay said, looking at Emily. "Why don't you wear what you were wearing that day?"

"I am," Emily told him.

The girls looked at each other. Emily was wearing a long grey cardigan, with sleeves that fell over her knuckles, over a long black top and skirt. It was the same thing she always wore.

"I thought that was your school uniform," said Kelly.

"No," Emily looked down at herself. "I'm not very on trend, am I?"

"So what?" Bethan said, hooking her arm through Emily's. "Look at me, I always wear black. Who wants to be a fashion victim anyway?"

None of them spoke on the bus as it trundled into town. Emily sat by the window, looking out at the streets as they slipped by, her dark eyes studying every brick, every nook and cranny, as if she were searching for her memories among the rubbish bins and rabble of shoppers. Bethan was sitting next to her, her arms folded, glaring at every passenger that walked by, like she was Emily's guardian.

Kelly found herself pinned into the window by Hashim. He didn't look at her or talk for the whole journey, but she could feel him next to her. It was a feeling she liked and disliked simultaneously.

Jay was standing, holding on to a pole, swaying with the movement of the bus, his eyes always on Emily, looking for any sign that she might be remembering something.

"Here!" Emily said suddenly. "We need to get off here."

The five of them piled off the bus and into the damp February afternoon. Kelly drew her parka tighter around her body and looked up and down the precinct where Hashim's family shop was. It was crucial that none of his family spotted him out of school. The bus had dropped them at one end of the pedestrianised precinct that was lined with the shops you would see on any high street. At the other end, four sets of double glass doors led into the Woodsville Mall, an indoor shopping centre with masses more shops of every type arranged over its four levels.

"You remember coming here?" Kelly asked Emily.

"We parked in the multistorey," Emily said. "Mum always liked to start in Primark, then Matalan, New Look and TK Maxx, and if we hadn't got everything we needed in those shops, she'd say we weren't trying hard enough. Mum loves a bargain..." Emily's smile faltered.

"Let's go," Jay said, and they headed across the precinct to Primark.

"Anything?" Hashim asked Emily as she walked around the piles and piles of clothes, her fingers trailing along the clothes racks.

"Mum bought a sundress for our trip," she said slowly. "It was blue with big yellow sunflowers on it. She loved it. She said it was a little bit of sunshine in a dress."

"And then what?" Kelly asked her. "Did she seem stressed or worried? Was she looking about as if she thought she was being followed or anything?"

Emily frowned. "No. If anything, she was happier than usual. We had two tickets to Spain, we were finally getting out of Woodsville. Mum told me…" Emily faltered and looked down at herself. "She told me it was going to be the last day that I ever wore black and grey. She laughed and said I always looked like I was going to a funeral, but that from now on everyone was going to see how pretty I was. She bought me…" Emily stared at a rail of dresses that had been marked down to five pounds.

"She bought me this," she said, picking up one made of white cotton that was printed all over with tiny green butterflies. "And a pair of green flip-flops to match. She bought me loads of things. When we left here, we had bags and bags of stuff."

"Where's all that stuff now?" Kelly asked, frowning. "We looked in your wardrobe, and your mum's too, and I didn't see that or loads of new stuff."

"I don't know." Emily looked puzzled. "Mum was always buying me bright clothes that I hardly ever wore – but I'd completely forgotten about all of that new stuff. I don't know where it is."

"So what did you do next?" Hashim asked her. "Another shop?"

"No, Mum said we'd already done a full day's shopping in one shop and we needed a break to get us going again. So we went to Costa. I had a cappuccino and a blueberry muffin. Mum had a cup of tea and a caramel shortbread."

Devoid of any cash, all five went and stood outside the coffee shop, while Emily peered in through the window. "We sat over there on that brown leather sofa," Emily told them. "We kept getting clothes out of the bags and looking at them. Mum said I'd look like a model. She said…" Emily dropped her gaze. "She said all the boys would fall in love with me. But that's Mum. She's always saying silly things to make me laugh. It was cold, really chilly and wet. It was only about three, but the sky was pretty dark already. Mum didn't want us to go home yet, so we decided to go and see a film at the Odeon. We'd never heard of it, but Mum said that looking at anything that wasn't Woodsville would be a plus."

Dragging their coats around them against the cold drizzle that sleeted into them, the five walked over to the Odeon foyer.

"We got popcorn and Cokes. The film was about this woman who was pretending that she wasn't in love with this man and she hated him, even though she didn't hate him and was actually in love with him all along. It was terrible, but it made us laugh. Mum laughs a lot. When we came, out it was properly dark and stormy. Mum asked me if I wanted to go to any more shops, but I said I'd had enough. So we got in the car and drove home."

"And you don't remember anything else?" Jay asked, disappointed.

"The next thing I remember is waking up at home and Mum not being there," Emily said. "This hasn't helped at all, has it?"

"Yes, it has," Jay told her. "You've remembered so much. We know that something must have happened between you leaving town and going home. We just need to work out what. Was there anything else?"

"We walked to the car park and got in the car. The traffic through the centre of town was awful; everyone was going home at the same time." Emily paused. "Mum decided to take the back way out of Woodsville. It was longer, but she reckoned it would be quicker. I can't remember getting home, or unpacking our shopping or having tea. I don't remember anything after we left the car park."

"Well, we need to go back the same way that you and your mum did then," Kelly said.

"You're right," agreed Jay. "But there's no bus that way which means…"

"We'll have to walk," Kelly moaned. "But it's miles!"

"Come on, Kel." Hashim draped his arm casually around her. "I'll prop you up."

"Not if you don't want your arm breaking," Kelly warned him, but with a sparkle in her eye.

They were laughing and joking as they made their way out of the centre of Woodsville and into the failing light of another grey day. But each was only too aware of the darkness falling all around them.

CHAP✝ER SEVEN✝EEN

"*T*his is doing my head in," Kelly said as they finally left the town centre and began making their way around the ring road. "And my feet are killing me."

"Imagine if your feet could really kill you," Hashim said. "Mutant, murderous feet in slingbacks – that's a horror film right there. Hey, look at that!"

"What?" Kelly asked.

"The street lights. They're going out." Hashim looked ahead where the lights burned bright orange, glowing haloes against the gloom, and then back where they had been walking. Not a single one was on.

"Wait here a sec," he said, holding Kelly back. "Just wait."

The pair of them watched as Emily and the others walked forwards into the next amber pool of light on the pavement. The moment they stepped under the lamp post, it fizzled and flickered, and the second they went past, it blinked out.

"Do you see anything… ghostly?" Kelly whispered, clutching Hashim's hand as she looked around.

"No, nothing, but that doesn't mean anything. I've never seen anything round Emily yet, but that doesn't stop a hell of a lot of spooky stuff happening, does it?"

"They haven't noticed anything weird. We should tell them," Kelly whispered, enjoying standing alone in the dark with Hashim more than she was ready to admit.

"No." Hashim shook his head. "We don't want to freak Emily out even more. Let's just walk behind and keep an eye on things."

As they picked up their pace again, Hashim realised that Kelly was still holding his hand. He squeezed her fingers.

"Are you planning to break my arm?" he asked her.

"Not yet," she said, glancing sideways with the briefest hint of a smile. "I'm scared and confused, and I've got a feeling that something really bad is going to go down, so for now, holding your hand is OK. I'll let you know if I change my mind."

Hashim nodded and even in the dark, even with Emily walking towards a memory that could not possibly be good, he couldn't help but feel happy knowing that Kelly King's hand was in his.

*   *   *

"Anything coming back, Emily?" Jay was walking just behind Emily who was arm in arm with Bethan. Despite the freezing chill, she didn't seem to be feeling the cold like the rest of them. If anything, she seemed amazingly calm and still.

"I remember us singing," she said. "Mum used to sing these old songs from when she was young. We were singing at the tops of our voices and it was raining, really coming down in sheets. It was like the wipers cleared the windscreen for about a second before you couldn't see anything any more, and then..."

Emily stopped underneath a flickering street light and looked down at the thick undergrowth that made up the centre of a sort of huge roundabout, the ring road ascending over it and another small road looping around it.

"What?" Kelly asked. "Do you remember something?"

Emily shook her head. "Nothing," she said. "From here, there's nothing. There's just... nothing."

"Your memories are still blocked," said Jay. "That might mean that we're getting closer to whatever happened. If we just keep going a bit more then—"

"No, after here there's nothing," Emily said. "This is where it ends."

"I don't get it. What do you—?" Jay stopped talking as the streetlight that had been flickering above their heads went out. Then each light, as far as they could see, blinked out in turn, leaving the surrounding area pitch-black. And with the darkness, all sound seemed to cease, the wind dropped and even the rain seemed to fall without making a noise.

"Down there," Hashim said, nodding into the undergrowth. "Look."

"There's a light in the bushes."

"It'll be pikeys," Kelly whispered. "They're always stopping down there till the council move them on."

"No, it's Mum." Emily spoke softly. "It's Mum. She's waiting for me down there."

"No, Emily, wait." Hashim stood in front of her. "What would your mum be doing down there? Whatever is down there, it isn't your mum."

"It is." Emily was certain. "I can feel her. Like she's inside of me and this… this is where she wants me. I need to go to her."

"Emily, don't! *Wait!*"

But Emily ran into the thicket without looking back.

"Well, we've got to go after her, haven't we?" Hashim said.

When the others said nothing, he led the way down into the undergrowth.

They descended in silence, the darkness almost solid in its blackness. The light ahead glowed steadily, pulsating slightly, like a beating heart.

"Emily!" Hashim suddenly shouted, making everyone jump out of their skins. "I just want to get her back here with us," he said. "There's something out there. Something that is most definitely *not* Emily's mother."

"Can you see something?" Jay asked in a whisper.

"No, but I can feel it. It's like a vibration in my chest and my bones. Don't you feel it?" The others shook their heads.

"It's like energy. It's like it feels when I see a ghost, only times by about a million."

"That sounds like a lot of dead people," observed Jay, the tone of his voice not quite matching his bravado.

"I think I can feel something too. It's getting hard to breathe, like the air is full of pollution," Kelly hissed. "Something bad is here. Something angry... something that wants to hurt Emily. Wants to hurt *anything*. We need to get to her. *Emily!*" This time Kelly screamed her friend's name in the darkness.

"Emily, come back! Whatever you think you feel, it's a trap! You need to get back here now, before it's too late!"

There was silence in reply. It felt as if the whole world was holding its breath.

And then they heard Emily scream, a knife-thin wail that cut through the night. "Help me!"

Hashim ran towards the sound with Kelly in his wake, the pain in her feet numbed by fear and adrenalin.

"We're coming! Hold on!"

Bethan and Jay started after them too, running into the thicket at the sound of the scream, but after only a few seconds, the undergrowth became so dense that they could not go forwards, left or right – or even backwards. And Hashim and Kelly were nowhere to be seen.

"What just happened?" Jay asked Bethan. "Where did they go?"

"I don't know," Bethan breathed, her head whipping round as she peered into the darkness. "One minute they were right here, and then there was the scream, and it was like the dark just swallowed them up. And us."

"Did you see anything? Hear anything?" asked Jay.

"Nothing," Bethan said and the two stood side by side, trapped on all sides by impenetrable darkness.

"You know, whatever it is that exists in the shadows in Weirdsville," Jay whispered. "It's real. It's out there. And it's coming."

Hashim and Kelly stumbled to a halt as they found Emily standing alone, a look of terror on her face, staring all around her.

"Emily, you're..." Kelly couldn't finish the sentence. She didn't know how to describe what she was seeing. Emily was glowing, giving off a faint light that merged into the air around her.

"Don't move," Emily told them, her voice cracked with terror. "What are they, Hashim? What do they want with me? I want my mum."

"Who's what?" Kelly asked, looking around, trying to make out what Emily was talking about.

"Them." Hashim nodded at the shadows and in that instant, Kelly could see what he could. People, loads and loads of people, all ages, all shapes and sizes, all colours and all of them, each and every one, dead. They just stood there, a crowd of hollow-eyed ghosts staring at Emily, no expression on their deathly faces, yet filling the night with emotion so that the air around them seemed to burn with fury.

Hashim swallowed, bracing himself against the flow of dead energy that threatened to engulf him.

"They aren't here to make friends, are they?" Kelly gasped, shrinking as a hundred pairs of lifeless eyes swivelled to not look at her.

"Ghosts," Hashim forced the word out. "Dead, angry souls. Hundreds of them. Not like anything I've ever seen before. And they're after Emily. They want to make her one of them."

"I just want to go to my mum," Emily begged as if she could reason with the figures that began to press and close round her.

"Remember what Jay's grandad said about the dead

never leaving Woodsville? Maybe this is what he meant. The dead, waiting in every shadow, waiting to… I don't know what they're waiting for, but for whatever reason, they want Emily."

"They're getting closer," Emily shrieked. "They're going to take me and I don't want to go with them. Help me, *please*!"

"Leave her alone!" Kelly felt the anger and grief of a thousand dead souls as she pushed her way through the freezing maelstrom of energy. The taste and smell of death filled her mouth and nose, while fear's icy fingertips squeezed her heart and tore at her lungs. Determined to make it to Emily's side, she staggered forwards, flailing her arms to beat off what could not be touched or held.

Finally she reached her friend. "Back off, you dead freaks!" Kelly yelled, feeling the most frightened and most foolish she ever had all in one go.

To her amazement, the swirling mass of dead halted and she realised that Hashim was also standing next to her. He seemed to be the focus of their anger now.

"Retreat or I will destroy you!" he shouted, his face full of fight.

Kelly raised her eyebrows. "You will?"

"Just go with me here, Kel," Hashim hissed, then raised his voice again. "You know my name. I am Hashim Malik, Destroyer of Evil, Destructor of Malice, Protector of

Innocence. Leave this place now or leave this world forever. One more step and I'll consign you to the void where you will be eternally nothing."

"Seriously?" Kelly whispered.

"She belongs to us," a thousand decaying voices rasped at once, words that Kelly and Hashim felt rather than heard. "Come to us and make us stronger. Come and be part of a new world, a dead world."

"God, you're stupid as well as ugly," Kelly spat out. "Why would anyone sign up for that?" She shrank back as the darkness massed around her and the voices whispered, "You next."

"Jay!" Bethan grabbed hold of Jay's arm as first one figure and then another and another emerged from the shrubs that imprisoned them. "Jay, they're actual ghosts, aren't they?"

Jay nodded, unable to quite believe what he was seeing, more frightened than he had ever been in his life, but also fascinated and excited. Ghosts were real; spirits could live on after death – it was a fact and he had to be one of the very few people in the whole world to witness it with his own eyes. Ghosts were real. Scary, menacing, strangely organised ghosts were real, like an army of the dead. He remembered what his grandad had said about the souls of Woodsville getting caught in the branches, unable to cross over, doomed to some dark fate that he would only hint at. Then Jay remembered quite quickly to be scared.

"Wha... what do we do?" Bethan asked him. "Didn't you say that ghosts can't actually hurt you? You did, didn't you?"

Jay felt his own spirit wither and shrink as he looked into expressionless faces that seemed to project so much negative emotion without ever changing.

"I said as far as I know, but actually... I know nothing about this."

"So what do we do?" Bethan urged as the crowd began to surge towards them.

"I'm sorry, Bethan. I have no idea."

"Emily!" The three of them turned towards another voice. The light had reappeared. It was stronger this time, glowing through the darkness, and the voice came from within. "I've been waiting such a long time for you. And they've been waiting for both of us. Emily, don't look at them, or touch them, or listen to them. I know what to do and together we'll be strong enough. Come to me and we can leave together."

"Mum!" Emily sobbed, stepping towards the voice. "Mum, I told them you were here! I told them you weren't dead! Why can't I see you?"

The light changed and Emily's mother stood before her.

"Take my hand," she commanded, holding out her glowing fingers. "Everything will be OK, you'll see."

"Are we going to Spain, Mum?" Emily asked.

"We're going somewhere better than Spain."

"No!" Hashim shouted. "No, Emily, don't do it. Your mum is dead, don't you see? She's a ghost too! If you go with her then…"

He tailed off as Emily took her mother's hand in her own, the dim light within her flaring like a candle the moment the two touched. Hashim and Kelly watched open-mouthed as Emily wound her arms around her mother's ghost and smiled.

"Let her go!" Hashim yelled, fear cracking his voice. "I'm the Destroyer of Evil! I'll send you back to the darkness and that other thing – the void! Let her go!"

A burst of light flared in their faces, knocking them both off their feet, and for a second, Kelly felt as if her whole body was burning up and twisting with agony. She heard a thousand and more angry screams tearing through her flesh. Then there was nothing. Then she was just lying on the wet, uneven ground with Hashim by her side.

A single dark figure stood before them.

"When we come for you, you will be all alone," it whispered, the words dragging across Kelly's skin like nails, before it vanished in an instant.

It took the two of them some seconds to gasp in enough air to be able to speak.

"What the hell happened there?" Kelly breathed.

"That ghost... that ghost took Emily," sobbed Hashim. Tears were running down his face.

"Emily's mum, you mean?"

"I think... I think it killed her!" Hashim crouched on the ground, sobbing, hugging himself.

"No, that was Emily's mum. She was protecting Emily; she wouldn't hurt her. She was protecting her from all of the... whatever they were." Kelly wasn't certain what had just happened, but she was sure about that. In the second before the glowing figures vanished, she'd felt the love between them, almost as painful as the hate that had been palpitating in the surrounding darkness.

"Where is she then?" Hashim shouted. "Where's she gone?"

"I... I don't know," Kelly said. "Maybe her mum got her away somewhere safe. But the main thing is those other angry ghosts – they've gone too." Kelly pushed the evil whispering to the back of her mind, uncertain whether Hashim had heard it too.

Suddenly new shouts broke the darkness. "Kelly! Hashim! What happened?" Jay and Bethan ran over, sliding on their knees in the mud.

Kelly and Hashim looked at each other.

"Did you see them?" Hashim asked Jay and Bethan, who exchanged a look that told him everything he needed to know.

"We tried to follow, but we couldn't find you and then they were all around us. It felt like they were sucking all of the air out of the night and then, just when we thought we'd had it, we saw a big light and they went, and you were here – just a few metres away the whole time. Where's Emily?"

"We don't know." Kelly felt the tears in her voice. "The ghost of her mum came and then she disappeared. At least, we think it was her mum. I don't understand what just happened. Why? Why were all those ghosts here after us? After Emily?"

"I don't know," Jay shook his head. "I always knew there was something, but nothing like that – it's like there are two towns existing in the same place at the same time, only one of them is full of ghosts. Ghosts who want something else, something more… but I don't know what or why."

"We can't think about that now – we have to find her," said Hashim, scrambling to his feet. "Emily!"

They ventured deeper into the dip until they were walking under the flyover. The steady hum of traffic vibrated above their heads.

"I can hardly see a thing," Bethan whispered, her nerve endings numbed with fear.

"Don't worry, they've gone for now at least," Kelly reassured her. "The lights are back on up there and it doesn't feel quite so, you know, heart-stoppingly freaky any more."

"We've got to find Emily," Hashim insisted. "We need to. If we don't then…"

"Then what?" Jay asked.

"Wait, look – what's that down there?" A little further down the slope, something glinted in the passing headlight of a car on the flyover. Scrambling down the last and steepest part of the descent, Hashim reached it first.

"Stop!" he called out. "Wait there."

"What is it?" Jay asked.

"It's a car," Hashim called. "It's a blue Ford Fiesta – at least it was. It looks like it's been in a fire."

"That's Emily's mum's car," Bethan whispered. "Oh my God!"

"Look!" Kelly reached up and pulled a swatch of something hanging from a branch. The piece of material was dirty and blackened, but even in the dark it was possible to make out the butterfly pattern. It was the dress that Emily had bought on the last day with her mother.

"Oh no! He's going to look in the car – Hashim, don't!" Jay called, but it was too late. Hashim had slid open his mobile phone, shining the light inside the car.

The others watched as he recoiled in horror, sliding in

the mud as he desperately tried to back away from the car, then retching on to the wet grass.

"We're coming!" Kelly, Bethan and Jay slid down to where Hashim was sitting shaking, staring at the burnt out wreck.

"She's in there," he managed to say at last. "Looks like she's been there for weeks. There's this smell of burnt stuff and rotting, but I can tell. It's definitely her."

"Emily's mum." Jay nodded. "She died in that car, and that's what she was trying to tell Emily all along. Somehow Emily got out, but the accident must have given her amnesia. No wonder she couldn't remember what had happened."

"That's not what happened," Hashim managed to say.

"Tell us, Hashim," said Kelly, putting an arm around his shoulders and looking into his eyes.

"There's someone else in there." Hashim closed his eyes.

Bethan felt her heart skip a beat. She knew what Hashim was going to say next.

"It's Emily."

CHAP✝ER EIGH✝EEN

"*I* haven't slept or eaten, and every time I close my eyes, I see them. I hear them… And I still don't understand what it all means," Kelly said, her fingers wrapped around a warm mug of tea that Jay had made her as they sat around his grandad's table.

It had been two days since they had found the car. Today was the first time they had met up since. They had gone to Albert's flat to try and make sense of it.

"She was a ghost. This whole time, Emily was a ghost." Hashim shook his head. "That's why she couldn't remember what happened to her mum, or what happened to her. She was dead, but she didn't know it. Just like that woman up the hall who's still trying to get into her flat. She didn't know it and… neither did we."

"Emily and that ghost aren't quite the same. That woman's a shadow – a memory in time," Albert said. "Emily must have gone so quickly she didn't have time to realise what had happened to her. Her spirit was confused, so she took herself to a place where she felt safe – her home. And that's how she got separated from her mother's spirit."

"But we all saw her," Bethan protested. "Not just Hashim. All of us, other kids at school. We saw her, we spoke to her. We *touched* her and everybody knows you can't touch a ghost!"

"You can," Albert told them. "You can touch a really strong ghost just as sure as you can touch that table. And they can touch you back too, if they want to. Emily must have been drawing her energy from you four. The closer you got, the stronger she became. Your friendship gave her form. Bet you noticed bulbs going, batteries draining, electrical faults when she was around. They can use electrical power to manifest."

"The lift that first night at Bethan's," Jay breathed.

"The DVD player and our phones," added Hashim. "And the photographer's battery."

"The street lights," Kelly said finally. "Going out one by one. I just can't believe it. I got to know her, to *like* her. You can't make friends with a dead girl."

"Dead or not, she was still the same person," Albert said. "You got to know her and you helped her. You reunited her with her mum and together they had the strength to go into the light, to cross over the way the dead should be able to. That's getting rare around here. Either you're stuck, you're nothing, like the woman in the hallway who is trapped dead energy, or those things take you. Emily might have been dead, but you saved her life. You saved her *after-life*."

"Albert, what were those things?" Kelly asked him, their final message to her still shivering in her guts.

"Lost souls," Albert said matter-of-factly. "Trapped souls. All this land around here used to be an ancient forest. Mile upon mile of it, for thousands and thousands of years. People knew better than to mess with it, to go in it or try to chop it down. Or at least they did until forty years ago. That's when they ripped it up and built Woodsville – and something's been leaking out ever since, some evil that's older than the universe. And it's getting stronger, spreading further. I've spent my whole life trying to push it back, a tiny bit at a time, but then I got old and lost my legs, and I couldn't do it any more. When your father wouldn't take up the fight, I thought the cause was lost."

Albert looked at Jay, then at the other three. "But now I'm not so sure. What you need to know is that the land around here feeds on the dead, keeps their souls trapped here in the darkness and the waiting shadows. There's an army of ghosts out there, thousands and thousands of them, and one day it will be us against them. The living versus the dead."

"Maybe we should move," Bethan suggested in a small voice, thinking of her uncle's caravan in Wales and how appealing it suddenly seemed.

"Wouldn't do you any good," Albert told them. "Woodsville's where it begins, but it won't end here. It won't end anywhere unless…"

"Unless what?" Jay asked.

"Unless you lot can stop it."

"How can we stop anything?" Kelly protested. "We're a bunch of kids off an estate!"

"You've stopped them once already," Albert reminded her.

"By accident – we had no idea what we were doing!"

"He did." Albert nodded at Hashim. "He might not know exactly what to do with it yet, but they knew what he might do. He's a destroyer of evil, and you, Kelly King, you're the warrior."

"I don't mind a fight," Kelly protested. "But I'm no warrior!"

"You are if you'll let yourself," Albert told her. "There's no braver or more powerful heart than yours."

"Oh, and what's my super power? Class boffin?" Bethan rolled her eyes.

"Partly, and partly your intuition. You'll always know what's coming next even if you can't stop it—"

"Rubbish!" Bethan scoffed. "I didn't know Emily was

261

dead. I didn't know there were a bunch of bad ghosts hanging around trying to kidnap her soul."

"Or *did* you?" Albert nodded, making Bethan sigh with exasperation.

"And as for you, young man." Albert looked at Jay. "You are Jason Solomon Romero, fifteenth generation ghosthunter. This is your destiny and it's time I taught you the skills your father should have."

Jay looked at his grandad for a few seconds. No matter how mad everything Albert was saying sounded, it was obviously the horrible truth and he had a million questions that he was terrified of hearing the answers to.

"Another cup of tea, Grandad?" he asked instead.

"This is all wrong," said Kelly angrily. "We noticed Emily more when she was dead than we did when she was alive. Now the police have the car and the papers have reported the accident. Everyone's talking about her like they were her best friends, like they weren't jeering and calling her names only a couple of weeks ago. It's like the whole school is lying! No one cared about Emily when she was alive. Not even us."

"But you cared about her when she was dead. You couldn't save her from death, but you saved her from Hell, and that's something that only true friends could do. Emily Night was very lucky to have you."

"There should be something, some proof that she was

here. That would make everyone see what's happening all around them. Wake them up to it and maybe even warn them. I know! The photo – Emily will be in the school photo! We know how long she's been dead and that the photo was only taken last week. That will prove to everyone that she was a ghost and that they all saw her!"

"It won't," Jay said, although he was reluctant to disappoint Kelly. "I thought of that already. I heard Bacon saying the proofs were back, so I sneaked into the school office and took one of the prints. Here." Jay took a photo out of his bag and handed it to Kelly.

She scanned the image until she found the four of them in the back row. There was an empty space where Emily had been standing. There wasn't even a shadow or the hint of a person there.

"So there's nothing, no proof that any of this happened at all," Hashim said miserably. "Apparently, the whole world is in danger from a load of hacked off dead people and no one but a bunch of kids and a senile old man know anything about it."

"Oi, less of the old," Albert warned him, but with a glint in his eye. All of this had certainly improved his mood, Jay noticed. Only his grandad could be cheered up by death and mayhem. "What matters is that you four know the truth, and when you know the truth, you don't need proof," Albert said. "And the next time, you'll be ready."

"I don't want a next time," growled Hashim. "I don't ever want to see or feel those things again."

"I'm afraid you might not have a choice," Albert said. "But when it comes, I'll be there to help you."

"Don't bother because I'm not going to be. I'm off to play footy." Hashim got up and stormed towards the front door.

"Hashim!" Kelly ran after him. "You OK?"

"Fine." Hashim couldn't look at her. "I'll see you around sometime."

"But I thought we—?"

Hashim slammed the door shut behind him.

"He'll be OK," Jay told the girls as they stepped out of the lift. "It'll take a while. He saw a lot of stuff that we didn't and he feels more than us. But in the end he'll come round. You'll see."

"I hope so," Kelly said in a small voice, reluctant to admit even to herself that Hashim had turned out to be someone she liked and who mattered.

"And what about us?" Bethan asked. "Will we just go back to how we used to be? Not speaking to each other. Not being friends."

"I don't think we could even if we wanted to." Kelly put an arm round her. "And I don't want to, do you?" Bethan shook her head.

"Look, we helped Emily in the end. We did what we set out to do and I bet that wherever she is, she's thanking us."

"I'm just hoping for a little less weirdness for at least a bit," Bethan said. "A bit of maths homework and *Deal or No Deal*. That's what I want right now."

"Yeah, or Andrea Clarkson going on and on about her latest boyfriend," Kelly laughed.

"Or hours and hours on the internet looking up proof of aliens – that's what I'm going to do," grinned Jay.

"Only you would think that's not weird," Bethan teased.

The three friends smiled at each other.

"See you later," Kelly called over her shoulder as she walked off with Bethan, and Jay found that despite everything, he was extraordinarily happy to realise that was true. He *would* see Kelly later. She was a part of his life now, and even an army of the dead and the imminent end of the world couldn't spoil that.

Jay whistled to himself as he walked round a corner, slap bang into someone. He looked up to find a boy staring intently back at him. Jay gawped. The other boy had his hair, his eyes, the same freckle on the end of his nose. The other boy was definitely him. He had bumped into himself.

"I've been waiting for you," he told himself. "You need to come with me now. There's not much time."

"Er…"

"Yeah, yeah, I know it's freaky. I know that the last person you needed to see today was me, I mean you, but anyway, you have to come with me now. It's your only chance."

"But you're..."

"You, yes, I know and I'm breaking the laws of time and space to try and save everyone's life. Come with me now and there's a chance that you might not die. It's a small one, but hey."

Jay stared into his own eyes and saw that whatever else this person was doing, he was not lying.

And then he turned on his heel and he ran.

Four freak accidents…
  Four mysterious deaths…
    Four signs of trouble…

      Is it coincidence?
    Or is it just really bad luck?

Welcome back to Weirdsville

Read on for a sneak teaser…

CHAPTER ONE

"None of our business, I say." Kelly sprawled over the café table and leaned her chin into her hands, scowling. "Everyone who goes to Riverbank School for Girls is a right stuck-up cow anyway."

"That's one way of looking at it," Jay said, glancing warily out of the window, as if he were keeping watch out for someone. "But four girls from the same school getting squashed, decapitated, burnt and drowned in the space of a few weeks is not only horrible, it's also plain weird. And if it's weird, then it's our business."

"Is it?" Kelly buried her face in her hands. "Is it *really?* Can't we just forget about all that so-called destiny crap and get a DVD and a Chinese instead? Hashim's pretending that the whole thing with Emily never happened. Why can't we?"

Jay said nothing, his eyes fixed on the busy street outside.

"Look at this headline. The papers seem to think it's mass hysteria." Bethan spread a copy of *The Woodsville Gazette* out on the tabletop. The front-page headline read FOUR FREAK ACCIDENTS LINKED BY TEEN DEATH PACT?

"That's rubbish." Jay tore his eyes away from the window to look at Bethan. "I mean if you were going to top yourself you wouldn't *choose* to do it by drowning in a septic tank, would you?"

"Blergh." Bethan pulled a face. "Seriously gross."

"Even if this is something… *Weirdsville*," Kelly grimaced, "how exactly do you propose we get involved? How are a bunch of kids from Woodsville High going to get into Riverbank to find out what's going on? Because, just so you know, my breaking and entering days are over."

"We don't have to break in. Someone's asked us to go there." Jay glanced over his shoulder before looking back at Kelly who looked horrified.

"You what? Who? *Why*?"

"Um… that's sort of my fault," Bethan mumbled. "Since I wrote about what happened with Emily on my blog I've had a ton of comments – loads of people posting about weird stuff they reckon has happened to them. And last night I had an e-mail from one of the girls at Riverbank asking if she could talk to us. She thinks we can help her."

"You are joking me, aren't you?" Kelly growled.

As Bethan shook her head, a girl with smooth, long blonde hair sat down at the table and held out her hand to Kelly.

"Hello, I'm Charlotte Raimi. Thank you very much for meeting me. I didn't know who else to talk to."

Sitting back in her seat, Kelly glared at the girl's hand and folded her arms.

Charlotte Raimi dropped her hand and smiled tightly at Jay and Bethan. "We've tried to get help, but no one takes us seriously at all. They think we're hysterical."

"Mental, more like," Kelly muttered under her breath.

"You see, the girls that died – it wasn't by accident. They were cursed, every one of them. Cursed to meet a horrible death and…"

Charlotte swallowed, unshed tears glittering in her bright blue eyes. "And I'm going to be next."

To be continued…

Coming September 2010